CW00410657

A DOCTOR'S NOTES

BY THE SAME AUTHOR

The Harlequin Edition

A DOCTOR'S NOTES

Julian Fane

Book Guild Publishing
Sussex, England

First published in Great Britain in 2007 by
The Book Guild Ltd
Pavilion View
19 New Road
Brighton, BN1 1UF

Copyright © Julian Fane 2007

The right of Julian Fane to be identified as the author of this
work has been asserted by him in accordance with the
Copyright, Designs and Patents Act 1988.

All rights reserved. No part of this publication may be
reproduced, transmitted, or stored in a retrieval system, in any
form or by any means, without permission in writing from the
publisher, nor be otherwise circulated in any form of binding or
cover other than that in which it is published and without a
similar condition being imposed on the subsequent purchaser.

All characters in this publication are fictitious and any
resemblance to real people, alive or dead, is purely coincidental.

Typesetting in Garamond by
Keyboard Services, Luton, Bedfordshire

Printed in Great Britain by
Antony Rowe Ltd, Chippenham, Wiltshire

A catalogue record for this book is available from
The British Library

ISBN 978 1 84624 112 3

CONTENTS

PART ONE

NOTEBOOK ONE

This notebook is the property of Dr Joseph Selaby of The Poor Cottage, Chantry Road, Maeswell, also of St John's Surgery, St John's Court, Maeswell. If found, please return it to one address or the other immediately. A reward for its safe return is on offer. The notes on these pages are private and confidential. Thank you.

The paragraph above is no doubt counter-productive. All the more reason not to lose my notebook. The medical records of my patients are kept in the Surgery, my notes refer to everything I cannot record, including personal matters. I am tempted to be indiscreet here. Probably another mistake, typical of me at the present time! I would read or at least look into a sort of diary if I found one. I would look into any document that I was told was private and confidential. I suppose I am more inquisitive than honourable. I am human, too, therefore might accept the reward. Yes – human – unfortunately.

Maeswell is a town in the South of England. It is large enough to support two doctors' practices. St John's Surgery, of which I am a partner, boasts three other doctors, Cunningham, Woods and

Audrey Fletcher, a young lady doctor, and two nurses, Annie Miller and Nicky Benning. We treat an enormous number of patients from a wide catchment area of town and surrounding villages.

Two months ago I came to live in Maeswell in order to get away from overwork in a hospital, from an overcrowded city, from love that was over, and to be nearer my mother. I should rearrange those motives in the order of their importance.

Mrs Symonds brought me another ailment today, a bruised heel of her right foot, which caused her to hobble into my consulting room with aid from Nurse Annie. We are already more than acquaintances – she has come to see me each week since I have had my brass plate on the door. She is a widow, an OAP, lonely but popular, and leads an active social life of the elevenses description. I have become a socio-medical port of call, as Drs Cunningham and Woods apparently were before me. I was about to speed her on her way this morning when she said: 'If I'm not careful, Doctor, you'll be thinking I'm a hypochondriac.' Wind was thus taken out of my sails. I paid more attention to her heel and diagnosed that it would soon be better. She was duly grateful and walked out with no trace of limp.

I am forty and unattached, my sister is older than me, my mother is seventy-five and a widow, and my father died ten years ago; but I prefer not to think about time and its passage. Besides, statistics lie. Here is a true statement: I am old enough – old enough to value my parents, be sorry for things, have regrets, and to know better. My father was a doctor, and my mother a nurse – I inherited my profession. I remember Father when he was old – he would be ninety if he were alive today – white-haired, bespectacled, with a white moustache, upstanding, and a solid down-to-earth shape. He was not an intellectual, and had no culture to speak of. He was also obstinate, opinionated, impatient, peppery, and not easy to live with. He adored Mother and drove her half-demented, was devoted to his children and exasperated them, and was unshakeably loyal to all of us, and to friends, colleagues, staff, and political party. He was not quite what he appeared to be. He was English, perhaps Celtic, and comparable to an iceberg that is bigger beneath the sea than above it. He had two talents that are rarely combined, common sense and vision.

By 'vision' I mean seeing deeper than surfaces, and foresight.

I am glad to pay him overdue compliments here. I never praised him verbally.

Dr Frank Cunningham, the senior partner in this practice, is slightly reminiscent of Father. He must be past retiring age. He is the traditional 'country' doctor, rosy-checked, bluff, with a loud voice and usually attired in a tweed suit. He is a 'racing' man – he goes to horse-racing meetings with his sparky little wife. He inspires awe, and could scare the hell out of diseases.

Dr Denis Woods is the opposite type, plump, an accessible roly-poly, and a jokey family man who refers to his good-humoured wife as 'the Queen Mother' and to his four boys as 'the gladiators'.

Dr Fletcher differs from the other two not only by sex, but also because she is idealistic. She is not cynical about medicine and its limitations – she winces when Dr Cunningham in our rest-room announces that we doctors understand no more than twelve per cent of human physiology. She believes she knows more than that, she believes in science and its advances, she is a refreshing individual with energy, shining eyes, a husband and two children. She is not acquainted with failure.

Annie and Nicky are excellent nurses: you can tell they are because of their cheery attitude to their work – nurses cannot be noticeably sentimental or glum. Nicky is the younger one, and I find her propinquity distracting.

Three awkward sessions with this morning's patients. First, an unaccompanied child came into my consulting room, a teenage girl. I shook her hand, asked her name, sat her down, and returned to my chair.

'Are you here for your mother?' I asked.

Her name was Kathy Leonard and I had treated Mrs Leonard for blood pressure.

'Not really,' Kathy replied, blushing. She is a brown-haired sweet-looking girl.

'Do you need help?'

'Can I shut the door?'

'I'm afraid not. The rule is that I have to keep the door open if I'm alone with a member of the opposite sex.'

'There are people in the passage – they'll hear me.'

'I'll call a nurse in, then we can shut the door.'

Kathy looked negative, but I buzzed for Nicky. Rules apart, I thought she was going to cry.

Nicky joined us and the door was closed.

'What is it, Kathy?' I asked.

'Can I have the pill?'

'How old are you?'

'Sixteen.'

Nicky said: 'Think again, Kathy – I've seen you with your mother – you're younger than that, aren't you?'

'No.'

I said: 'I could ask your mother, Kathy.'

She burst into tears and blubbed out: 'I don't want a baby, and I'll lose my boyfriend if I won't let him. He's told me it's either.'

'My advice for you is get rid of that boyfriend without delay and find a better boy.'

She cried harder.

Nicky said: 'You're fourteen, aren't you, Kathy, you're underage?'

She shook her head.

'Dr Selaby can't prescribe the pill for you. Okay – you don't want your parents to be involved – you do want to cling on to your boyfriend. Tell him to buy a condom in a gents' toilet.

Tell him to control himself and stop being selfish.'

She fled. Kathy ran out of my room, slamming the door. Nicky and I pulled faces at each other, and she ushered in my next patient.

He was a boy, ten or so, with shorn head jailbird-and-footballer style, and mother in attendance, who had made the appointment. She is Mrs Wilkinson and he is called Dylan. She is a hefty female with a loud voice.

'Dylan's fell on his head and I'm here so you can check him over,' she said.

'Where did you fall, Dylan?' I asked.

'Down the Rec.'

'Did you fall over or fall from a height?'

'He was on the swings,' his mother bellowed.

I examined his head and saw a swelling.

'When did this happen?'

Early, according to Mrs Wilkinson.

'When did this happen, Dylan?'

'Going to school.'

'You stopped to have a swing on the way to school?'

Mrs Wilkinson objected: 'What's wrong with that?'

'Did you lose consciousness, Dylan?'

'Saw stars.'

'Are you clear in your head now?'

'Yah.'

'Who's sitting on the throne of England?'

Mrs Wilkinson answered angrily: 'He won't know a thing like that – he doesn't do history.'

'Where are the Houses of Parliament, Dylan?'

He suggested on a querying note: 'New York?'

I said to Mrs Wilkinson: 'He seems not to know much.'

She replied: 'He wouldn't have known before he fell on his head – we're not your sort, Doctor – and I didn't bring Dylan here for you to make him look stupid.'

'Well,' I replied, 'I think he's none the worse for his fall. His head's mostly bone in my opinion.'

Mrs Wilkinson was mollified. She thanked me for my opinion, and nudged Dylan into saying, 'Ta!'

My third awkwardness was caused by the mother of a third child. Mrs Wainwright, a woman even bigger than Mrs Wilkinson, led in Rowena, aged five. Rowena had breathing problems, a chesty cough and chronic wheezing.

I said: 'She needs to lose weight, Mrs Wainwright.'

'That's as may be, Doctor, but shouldn't you examine her?'

'I can examine her from where I'm sitting. She's pounds overweight. Come back when she's slimmed down.'

'You do surprise me, Doctor. She's got puppy fat. You're not kind to tell her to slim.'

'I was telling you to take more care of your daughter's health.'

'Oh, I am mortified. I am, Doctor Selaby. Come along, Rowena – you can have your ice-cream now.'

The Poor Cottage is a misnomer, it cost a lot.

I had a fine flat in London, in St John's Wood, but I gave it away and started again from scratch down here. The Poor Cottage has two of the most desirable features of property today, it is within walking distance of my place of work and it has a garage. I also like its location, in a quiet sidestreet, its age and charm. It is the last dwelling in a terrace of five, semi-detached, partly tiled on the outside, and inside has two receps, two bed, one bathroom, a kitchen and a small walled garden – the garage is a modern addition. The rooms are small and low-ceilinged, the walls are thin and damp rises; but I can make it warm and find it cosy. And being near my mother saves trouble.

Besides, it is nice for me and I hope for her. She has been an excellent mother to me, and to Jane, although Jane feels I was the favourite. I believe Ma always did her best to be fair and unoppressive: which is a considerable compliment considering her strong personality. She was born Catherine Weight, daughter of a Norfolk farmer. She must have been attractive, tall, good-looking, humorous. She met her match in hospital in Norwich – Father worked there. He soon set up in private practice. She became his nurse and receptionist as well as the mother of two children. She put Father first, and vice versa – their parental policy was to send Jane and me to boarding schools and give us as much time as they could spare in the holidays. No complaints, no regrets – I had a good boyhood and youth. The crunch

10

came when Father died. She drew her own conclusions from the facts: Jane was married to Neil Proctor, also a farmer in Norfolk, they had two children, and were working night and day in order to make ends meet, and I was too busy to visit her. She sold the family house in Suffolk and moved down to Maeswell, where she had a friend. When the friend died, I left London and also came to Maeswell. Now I can look in on her often – her flat in Silver Court is reasonably close to my cottage. Today's visit was exceptional: she dredged up the subject of Iris. She said that The Poor Cottage would not have been a worthy home. I thought I showed she had given offence – she took no notice. Fear it may be a sign of her mind fraying at the edges.

My colleague Audrey stirs nostalgia in me. I used to feel as she does. I followed in Father's footsteps not exactly to please him or because he influenced me – those reasons were superseded by my own enthusiasm. I read about the 'first' European physician, the Greek Hippocrates, and was struck by the most famous of his *Aphorisms*: 'Life is short, Art long, Occasion sudden and dangerous, Experience deceitful and Judgment difficult.'

I still agree with every word of the Hippocratic oath, so-called. Professionally, after I had got the better of my squeamishness, my curiosity was satisfied by practice of the art of diagnosis and my philanthropic instincts by the aim of healing the sick. But London, my hospital in London, my life in London, reduced me to the point of wishing to be elsewhere, in a provincial setting, as far as possible from the rush and bustle and the old friends. I was able to buy myself into St John's Surgery – I had enough money for that, my cottage was bought with a mortgage. The change seems to be having some of the desired effect – I go to work every day almost willingly.

Frank Cunningham invited me to dinner. He is a dear old boy and has been kind to me. He lives with his wife Penny in a 1950s house in a garden at Larkspur, the swish part of Maeswell. The house is called Chandos. It is furnished like a four star hotel. Penny is a dear of a different sort: she has not settled for being in her late sixties, has a curly blonde hairdo, is exuberant and flirty, and makes unmalicious jokes at Frank's expense. Dignified men often seem to drive their wives to ragging them in public. The other guests were our Protestant parson, William Wetherby, an OAP, with ailing wife Ada, and Patricia Deacon, thirtyish, unmarried, toothy and works for the Council. We ate in the dining-room – formally furnished with mahogany and a pair of prints of Montague Dawson yachts sailing the seas. I sat between Penny and Patricia: Penny said to Patricia and me as she indicated the seating, 'I hope you two get on together or even get off.' The food was soup, fish pie, prune jelly in a mould, cheddar cheese, and milk chocolates. It was served by a superannuated maid wearing a scarlet dress with pinny and odd upstanding

12

headgear: Penny proudly announced that she had invented the uniform. We drank or at least were offered three wines, white, red and port. Penny jumped up to serve and replenish glasses: she said Frank had no palate and the amazing thing was that he was able to speak. The conversation was meant to be general, but Penny talked so much that she inhibited the rest of us. Moreover, the Reverend Wetherby's graces at the beginning and end of the meal discouraged jollity. We left early: Frank had revealed that in the old days of country entertainment carriages were ordered at ten o'clock. Both Cunninghams thanked us for having accepted their invitation. They clearly love Chandos and live there happily, but it is not convenient – they have to have two cars, one for Frank, another for Penny to reach the shops.

Ma has apologised for again delving into my past.

Dinner party food does not suit my digestion. Father used to say that amateur cooks were killers, and now almost everybody is an amateur cook, having a bash at esoteric sauces and mixing up flavours. Penny Cunningham's dinner was good, but I have reason to believe I can have too much of a good thing.

Mrs Symonds' heel has moved to her hip, so she tells me. She resisted my attempts to laugh it off. She demanded an x-ray, and, to save time,

I referred her to Radiology in St Anne's Hospital in Tinbury. Poor NHS!

I dare to tell patients not only to eat less but also to drink less. I cave in not only to Mrs Symonds, but also to the people who seem to queue up to beg me to intervene on behalf of battered wives, bullied children, family finances and public safety. But the chances I get to do so are rare: the guilty parties run away and hide from doctors who might scold them. When I have managed to say my piece and wag my finger, I am forced to listen to the hackneyed record: 'My drinking is under control – I can stop when I wish to – I'm more amusing when I've had a couple – I drive better with a drink in me – it's not my fault – mind your own business, get out before I smash your face in, go to hell, I'll never speak to you again.'

Doctors, self included, are apt to respond feebly to such tirades, not just to avoid unpleasantness. They can make matters worse for those who have suffered and told tales. They cannot truthfully say excessive drinking is bad for everyone: some drunkards are kept alive after a fashion by pickling themselves in booze. Regrettably, it could be said, alcohol does not kill its addicts soon enough. And the fact is that 'cured' dipsos are often neither so healthy nor so nice as they were before the demon got its claws in them.

A surly girl barged into my consulting room and

said: 'Smear!' When I said, 'I beg your pardon?'
she repeated in a louder voice with the vulgar
modern intonation, 'Smear, smear,' as if to a
deaf person or a lunatic. I kept my temper, sat
her down, dragged her name etc out of her, and
again asked her to tell me slowly why she had
come to see me. My assumption was that she
was asking for the gynaecological test. She
deciphered 'smear' for my benefit largely by sign
language – pointing at her ear: she had been
trying to say, 'It's my ear.' She had earache, which
I was able to relieve.

The moral of a true story is that the government
of this country or whatever is left of it – England,
shall we say? – should urgently and forcefully
teach elocution and deportment. The 'smear' girl
spoke a language I could not understand, and
she slouched in such a way that I could foresee
her spinal and pelvic tribulations. Regional accents
have been put in the shade by the inverted snobs
who try to talk common, by a new type of
pidgin that elides words and is spoken with an
open mouth, and by the mystifying effect on
verbal communication of Hollywoodese,
Atlantese, popese, thugese, and the sloppiness of
liberalism. And a large percentage of English
people no longer deport themselves, they slouch
or waddle, shuffle or strut or mince

My notes were meant to stick to facts. Judgmental
I did not want to be, and the quagmire of politics
I hoped not to fall into. Yet I have to ask, if
only to ask myself, if ignorance was always a

15

defining trait of the Anglo-Saxon race. The French think so, but may be biased. A worrying number of my Maeswell patients fail to give me reassuring answers to the question. They have no understanding of ill health or probably of health, of my diagnoses and prognoses, or of how much danger they could be in. They talk of heart attacks when they have had strokes, and vice versa. Another possibly concussed boy was brought in to me the other day, and I asked him if he knew the name Adolf Hitler. The boy said Hitler had been Prime Minister long ago.

I have a rich patient, who has offered to enrich me. Tucker Bee – trade name or alias – was born and bred here, is now old and ill and has bought a house in Larkspur. He means to live in it as long as I can let him, and be buried with his parents in the graveyard near my cottage. He made his money in secondhand cars. He has a mistress/companion/secretary called Heather, who must be half his age. He called me out for a reason that was new to me. He said he was not ready to 'go' – 'I can play the market in bed.' He came to the point. 'Here's a codicil to my will. I testify on this bit of paper that you'll inherit from my estate one thousand pounds for every week you will have kept me alive from this day onwards. Is it a deal?' My reply was negative, and his comments were: 'You're no businessman. I may have a year or two or three. You're kissing away fifty-two thou per annum.' We parted on friendly terms. I think he knew that I knew he had a shorter life expectancy, and if I had agreed he would have demanded constant attendance. Tucker is a rogue – his name is roguish – amusing too.

I work longer hours than Frank Cunningham because I am younger than he is, and more hours than Denis Woods and Audrey Fletcher because they have children and I have none. Our agreement is that I shall work less if or when a fifth doctor is needed and joins the practice. I had no objection to these terms – I needed to be busy. And I am busy, if less so than I was in London. But spare time can be hard to fill. I must recover my love of reading one day. There are limits to how far one can walk. I hate most of TV. And I have no close friends here. These notes fill gaps.

Winter is on the way – the nurses have been doling out flu jabs.

Dined with Denis and the 'Queen Mother', his wife Alyson, who is as jovial as he is. They are in their late forties, and a great contrast to the Cunninghams. They live out of town, at Deacon's Holding, a farmhouse in a few acres of land on the outskirts of the village of Clayburn. My fellow-guest was Nicky Benning, who seems to me too attractive to be a nurse. We were softened up with dry martinis in the sitting-room – Denis was proud of his recipe for martinis, two tablespoonfuls of Noilly Prat to one bottle of Gordon's gin thoroughly shaken with ice. The sitting-room is cosy with its blazing fire, sofa and chairs with broken springs, pile of children's toys in a corner, and friendly old spaniel. Alyson, off stage, shouted that dinner was ready, and we joined her in the kitchen and sat at the table laid for four – the Woods' 'gladiators' were absent at school or elsewhere. The food was Irish Stew cooked in and served from a pail-sized pot, apple tart with cream from Alyson's Jersey cow, and hot cheese straws – all very tasty. We drank claret in alarmingly large wine glasses. The atmosphere was relaxed, which was not surprising in view of the alcoholic refreshment. Alyson is fresh-faced verging on ruddy, Denis looked ever more rubicund as the evening progressed, and Nicky sparkled at me in spite of my attempts to regard her repressively. Denis said that Alyson would have preferred him to be a vet because of her farm animals, and she said the best thing about him being a doctor was that he came in handy at lambing time. Denis told a good story with apologies for it having no end. Friends of a patient of his, a married couple, were going on holiday in France with their caravan. They were taking his aged mother along. They drove from their house in North Wales to Dover, where the old lady discovered that she had forgotten her passport. They told her not to worry, she could shut herself into the lavatory in the caravan and nobody would be any the wiser. The two younger people got through Passport Control and on to the cross-Channel ship. But towards the end of the voyage the lady in the lavatory was taken

18

ill. She was persuaded to stay where she was until they were through the French controls – they could contact a French doctor later on in France. There was no trouble in Calais, until they looked into the lavatory and were horrified to find that his mother and her mother-in-law had died. They returned to the *Douane*, confessed their crime, wringing their hands, and led the *Douaniers* back to where the caravan was parked. It plus the deceased and their car had vanished, they had been stolen.

On Sunday I took Communion at St Peter's, the church near my Poor Cottage. William Wetherby, whom I met at the Cunninghams' dinner, officiated with minimum fuss. Denis Woods had urged me to look at the stained glass windows.

Referred two lovely people to specialists for tests, and wish I believed that the members of my profession knew more than twelve per cent of the science of healing.

Ma fed me yesterday evening. Mildly curried chicken mayonnaise and rice with cucumber in it, then oranges caramelised – she apologised for cold food in winter, but I said she had given me two of the best on her menu. She said she would like to cook for me more often, and in the next breath that she knew doctors hated to be pinned down for meal-times. I supplied reassurance, and she assured me that I was a good son. Her flat is one of fifteen in a block with a warden in attendance. Most residents are widows, one is an unlikely spinster, Miss Gabriella Shelby, a pretty soft-spoken septuagenarian, who is thought to have had her share of the spoils of the war of the sexes. Ma was funny about the latest arrival, a bachelor, George Mills, retired chartered accountant, no oil painting, and a shy mouse of a man. Obviously for the first time in his life he has aroused interest of a romantic nature. The ladies of Silver Court are courting him, quarrel over him, make scenes because he is nicer to one of them than to another, and invade his flat or try to at all hours. Consequently George has been transformed from one of nature's wallflowers into the cock of the walk. His head is held high, and he smiles at the world instead of trying to conceal his protruding buckteeth.

My oldest friend Robert, Robert Chimes, my age, like my brother, up and coming barrister, married and the father of two, stayed the night here. He was on his way to some Assizes, and was checking that I was still alive. He took me out to dinner at the King's Head. He does not approve of my 'burying myself in the back of beyond'. He sees Iris, and might have been hoping to remake our match. An unsettling visit.

Annie Miller, senior nurse, produced a casualty for me to look at before I began to see patients this morning. The man had a deep cut into his forearm, wound gaping but no longer bleeding. He asked me to put a stitch in it. He would not give his name. Description – mid-fifties, short, balding, wearing anorak, T-shirt, jeans, trainers, and walking with exaggerated limp.

'How was your arm cut?' I asked.

'Someone slammed a window on it,' he answered in words and accents that were almost impenetrable.

'What's wrong with your leg?'

War wound – he was an invalid – and 'on benefit' – paid a basic means of subsistence by the state.

'What's your name?'

He would rather not say – it was only the stitch he wanted. He also withheld his address.

I explained that the wound needed to be cleaned, that Annie could clean it and I could close it up, and he was in life-threatening danger otherwise, but that we would not treat a person refusing to identify himself.

He gave in. He was Jim Tye from a cottage in Clayburn. He had a wife who would be angry with him for having got in trouble in Maeswell, he had spent the night out so as to have the cut attended to before he returned home, and that was the gospel truth.

He was a liar. I saw through him. He had been on burglary bent. Nobody had slammed a window on his arm, he had broken a window, the glass had been thinner than he expected and a shard had cut his arm. He pleaded guilty to my charges. I insisted on examining his leg and could see nothing wrong there: Jim begged and besought me not to put his name on my computer as it might be spotted by his GP in Taylton, Dr Rees, who had certified that he was unfit for work and worthy of financial support by tax-payers. Dr Rees would find out that he had walked in from Clayburn, Jim said, and that he was walking the five miles back – he would lose his 'benefit' and might as well be dead.

Annie and I put our heads together. It was our turn to give in. Against our principles we did as we were told by the criminal. Alas, the Welfare State!

As Father was a doctor and Ma a nurse, strange that I did not become a revolting dropout.

Frank Cunningham's wardrobe tells a story. He wears a grey suit for work, a blue suit if he is lunching out or going out to dinner after evening surgery, occasionally a dinner jacket that seems to have turned green with age, a tweed suit for racing, a tweed jacket on Saturday mornings if there is no accessible race meeting, and a black suit for the funerals of his patients. The Cunninghams do not go racing at Ascot, but Penny dresses as if for Ascot's Ladies' Day when they go to a point-to-point. Frank's uniform as punter includes a battered and stained brown Trilby and outsize binoculars in an old leather case.

Dinner with the Fletchers: how am I to return the hospitality of my colleagues? They live in Smith Street which leads to Larkspur, in an end of terrace Edwardian house, with carports at side and in the front garden. Andy Fletcher works in a stockbroking firm, was once a rugger-player, a forward, and maintains a connection with the game. He is short, broad and losing his dark curly hair. Their children are Kathy aged ten and Trevor aged eight. The other guest – not Nicky Benning, thank goodness! – was April, a friend and contemporary of Audrey, an anaesthetist by trade rather than in the social sense. My arrival must have been almost a last straw – it was a weekday, Andy only just ready after commuting homewards, the children probably complaining of having their hair brushed, and Audrey putting finishing touches to cookery and cushions; but I was greeted warmly after the family had caught its breath. Andy offered white wine or 'something more serious' – I took white wine, he took whisky. The food was supermarket, and none the worse for that – pâté, breaded bits of lemon sole with tartare sauce and peas, salad of foreign fruits with ice cream. We drank more dry white wine, then a sweet wine. We ate on our knees in the sitting-room – apologies for the ambiguity of sentence. Audrey did everything with help from the children, beamed, sparkled and did not flag, although she had worked her six hours at Surgery. Andy is the pasha type, he snapped his fingers for service. He has a rugger-player's sense of humour: he said his missis was more doctor than housewife and that it was all he could do to stop her serving dinner to guests in a kidney bowl. Audrey is a fine person, but is not 'personal', at least she does not get 'personal' with me – her public persona is impersonal. Le Corbusier said that houses had to be machines for living in; Audrey's externals look like a machine for living in. Perhaps the point of Andy is that he can bulldoze through the machinery. His selfishness forces her to be the humble servant of her mate.

I need a woman – that is, a daily lady or housekeeper. More patients come to see me, and I never have time to clean The Poor Cottage.

Eureka! I made a sort of joke of the above at the Surgery, speaking to Mr Peele, retired builder, who looks after the fabric of our building and does the odd jobs. Thirty-six hours later Mrs Peele rang my doorbell and said she was willing to oblige.

Mr Peele is a gentleman of the oldest school, he introduced himself to me as Mr Peele. He is a strong-featured man wearing spectacles. Mrs Peele wore a hat the other evening. She is in her sixties, also bespectacled, with neat straight grey hair and charm of the reserved kind. She offered to help me – work and pay not mentioned. She arrives on Mondays, Wednesdays and Fridays at eight sharp, buys all the 'liquids' and dusters she requires, and leaves a note at the end of the week stating her expenses and earnings. She cleans and tidies everything, and begins to tell me the gossip of the town. For a change, I feel cared for.

24

Of course, my home is not homely without a
kind wife presiding. But The Poor Cottage is a
misnomer not only in a financial context: I am
quite rich in luck – healthy, in work, a householder,
in my forty-first year. And, luckily, I have started
to read again – for the last year I have read
nothing but advertisements of new drugs. The
book that caught my eye and my attention is
The Journal of a Disappointed Man by W.N.P.
Barbellion. The author's real name was Cummings
– he died young of Multiple Sclerosis in the
early nineteen hundreds. The title of his book
touched a nerve, although I am so much luckier
than he was.

Heather rang today.
   'Do I know you?' I asked.
   'I'm Tucker Bee's partner. He's sinking, Doctor.'
   'How bad is he?'
   'Awful – he has been for days – he can't
breathe, and he's sick – and won't let me ring
for an ambulance – and won't have anyone else
to help. I'm at the end of my tether, honestly I
am.'
   She was sobbing, and I said: 'Listen, when I
last saw him he tried to bribe me. I can't get
involved with bribery and blackmail. I could ask
my colleague Dr Woods to take over the case.'
   'No – it's you he's after – I'm too tired to
argue, but, Doctor, please! Tucker always was
bad about money – he's still gambling and telling

me he's losing the money he was leaving me in his will – and I don't want to be a pauper – sorry for saying so. Please!'

I caved in. For the third time I caved in against my will, first to Iris, then to Jim Tye, now to Heather. I was trained to temper science with mercy, not the other way round. I have disappointed myself.

Anyway, I saw Tucker and had him carted off to hospital. He was charmless even *in extremis*. Heather was embarrassed to have asked me to salvage her inheritance. She is a nicer woman than Tucker deserves, and she looked a wreck. She was grateful and kissed me goodbye, I hope not prematurely.

We are no longer a nation of shopkeepers, more's the pity. The 'little' shops are being squeezed out of business by cruel taxation and supermarkets. The Maeswell shops that sold useful merchandise are either being taken over by ladies selling cushions and trinkets in their spare time or turned into residential premises. Thank God for Bertha, my greengrocer, and Nigel, my butcher, and the strangely-spoken girls who sell my baker's bread – all are close by The Poor Cottage. I risk being recognised by my patients when shopping locally in preference to driving out of town to the mammoth stores where the chill air-conditioning blows along the aisles.

Mrs Peele and my colleagues have been giving me a crash course in the social fabric of Maeswell.

In a small town, society is easier to analyse than it is in the metropolis, although social life everywhere and always is roughly the same, levellers notwithstanding. Rank, down here, is represented by Lord Havior of Havior Place, his wife, surviving son and mother. The Cunninghams mingle with the Haviors, and Frank has told me of his affection for and sympathy with the family. The elder son of the present Lord and Lady died of cancer in his twenty-second year, and mourning him was aggravated by the fact that he had been given at least half the estate and they would be severely embarrassed by the cost of the tax on death, the death duty. There is a second younger son, but he is not altogether satisfactory for some reason. Lord Havior is apparently more or less incapacitated by his troubles; Lady Havior works in the Hospice of St Christopher where her son was nursed; and Lord H's mother, Helen Lady H, lives in the High Street and serves on numberless charitable committees. Mrs Gradwell-Taylor and such sub-grandees, Frank and Penny, for instance, are invited to Havior Place for occasional melancholy meals and functions.

Next best, after the Haviors, are the rich and especially the rich philanthropists. The anglicised Russian Minksofts, who, believe it or not, make their money by shipping coal from Poland to Newcastle, support worthy causes and sit at the top table; and another family of generous millionaires bearing a good old English surname, Sinopopolis, throw lavish parties at which all and sundry are made welcome. My various informants amuse me with their descriptions of those of us grubbing about under the upper crust. We are the 'classes', a term more or less invented by Karl Marx's teutonic passion for pigeonholes – I am quoting Denis Woods. Every creature of the human animal kingdom is struggling for status, and life is a bare-knuckle fight, according to comfortable peace-loving Denis, who has tried to read a Marxist tract or two. Doctors and other professionals are the top dogs, then come the politicians, then the middle-middle and lower-middle class, and then the masses, the class called 'working' although it has less ambition than the other classes and works less. Maeswell is not short of snobbery. Ma described a pretentious resident of Silver Court: Mrs De Villiers, living in a flat on the ground floor, was unwell, and another lady, who is unpretentious and lives in a flat on an upper floor, suggested a visit to the invalid, 'Would you like me to come down and see you?' The invalid replied: 'Not "down", dear, not "come down", "up" would be more appropriate.' Mrs Peele and her husband, who belong to the traditional artisan/craftsman class, have no respect for the lowest class. Frank said that his gardener, a peasant and proud of it, called the class he thought lower than his own 'rank Labour' – a slur on socialism. This gardener took exception to a contemporary and neighbour who won money in the Lottery and strode into the pub smoking a big cigar: 'You could see he was common.'

* * *

Doctors cannot be serious snobs. Illness recognises no pecking order. Pain is classless. A few exceptions, the inevitable awkward squad, prove the rule that patients in hospital are apt to get on well together. Health and strength make the difficulties. Leadership is a mixed blessing.

I have been entertained by my three colleagues. How am I to return their hospitality? Social life is a minefield.

Cold days, dark days, Christmas is coming.

Miss Shelby turned up at the Surgery, thanks to Ma. She is the Gabriella Shelby who also lives in Silver Court. She wanted a face-lift – another woman wanting one – and the name of a cosmetic surgeon. She made no bones about it and did not ask me not to tell my mother. She must have been a maneater, and I cannot be sure she is no longer on the prowl. She laughs a lot, has laughter in her speaking voice, and cheers a man up. She smiles, too, and shows an appealing set of her own teeth. She mocked herself and flirted with me simultaneously. 'Isn't it ridiculous, being so vain at my age? But God save us from women who aren't vain! It's no sin to be naughty if you still have something to offer. Women are capable of romance at any age – you'd know that because you're a knowing doctor – and I'm quite determined to be looked after by a male nurse on my death-bed. It's a woman's duty to be ready for love, isn't it? – ever-ready, say I. Now, would

29

I look better with a little hitch behind each ear?'
Her mannerisms were as good as a play. She
hangs her head, then raises it and looks alarmingly
straight into my eyes, then it was a sideways
glance, an inviting movement of her lips, a full-
throated laugh at some pleasantry of mine, a
long warm handshake, a compliment – 'Your
proud mother didn't exaggerate' – and a little
grateful pat in the region of my breast-pocket.

I beg pardon for paying Gabriella Shelby back-
handed compliments, and thank her on behalf
of my sex for keeping her flag flying. Women
also owe her gratitude, although the jealous cats
would disagree: for she champions them against
the feminists, who have done and are still doing
them more harm than good. I remember Robert
picking holes in Virginia Woolf's book, *A Room
of One's Own*, an early tract that has influenced
thoroughly modern women to desert husbands
and abandon their children. Robert had been to
the Woolfs' home in Sussex, Monks House in
the village of Rodmell, and told me that Virginia's
bedroom with the narrow bed and no creature
comfort was the most effective passion-killer he
had ever dreamed of in nightmares. That Virginia
and her husband Leonard had intercourse there
was unthinkable, Robert said. And he pointed
out that in spite of having that room very much
of her own, a wonderful thing for a woman
according to her book, she had committed suicide.
Feminism has won women rights, some needful,
others self-destructive, for instance the right to

drive buses and box other women, and the financial rights that put men off marrying them. Worst of all, the feminists have brainwashed women into thinking they are like men, can behave almost like men, and can fulfil their potential by burning their bras and acting macho. My experience would equate feminism with the contraceptive pill as good ideas that have had bad effects. Gabriella Shelby may be a little over the top, but she is more feminine than feminist and I love her for it.

Nearly all pills should carry a health warning, in my opinion, like packets of cigarettes. A wag spoke a true word about Viagra: that innumerable women of a certain age must be cursing its inventor. Another old fool wanted a prescription for Viagra a few days ago. I reminded him that his heart was none too strong and said that a resumption of sexual activity would be the death of him. He is or was a fox-hunting man and had recourse to the jargon of the sport to explain himself: he wanted to be able to kill his fox. I said the fox was as safe as houses, he would be killed long before he could catch it. He called me a puritan and said he would buy his Viagra in France, where love was legal.

These 'notes' could be called a meander through my mentality while I settle into a new life, or an aimless ego-trip. But who is going to call them anything? They are my 'dear diary' although dateless, my secret, safety valve and consolation.

Here, I can express thoughts and emotions that a GP is obliged to keep to himself. Nowadays, when night falls so early, I am not tempted to take the country walks that I enjoyed on fine autumn evenings, and I sit and scribble by the fire.

I am in my consulting room from eight-thirty in the morning to eleven, then visit patients in their homes and in the Cottage Hospital. I am back in my consulting room between four-thirty and six-thirty. That is my basic routine for the five working weekdays. Every fourth night I am the duty doctor and emergency telephone calls from my patients come through to me at The Poor Cottage – each of the other doctors takes a turn at night work. Every fourth weekend I am in my consulting room on Saturday morning and on call on Sunday. About once every six weeks I attend at Accident and Emergency in St Anne's Hospital in Tinbury.

Treated my youngest patient since moving out of harm's way. She is called Laura and is nine months old. She was brought in to my evening surgery by her parents, a pretty mother and a father of the clean-cut English type who is a postman. Laura has croup and I prescribed a couple of ancient remedies – no antibiotics at this stage. She is a charming girl and looked blooming in spite of a cough and a touch of fever. She has fair hair, the bluest and whitest of eyes, an intelligent regard and a beguiling smile. Jenny and Paul Maxwell, the parents, will ring me at once if they notice any change in her condition, and anyway ring me early tomorrow morning. Jenny had come into my consulting room clasping to her bosom a bundle of swaddling clothes. She was the stereotype of concerned motherhood, a picture of love in action. Paul was the image of a supportive paterfamilias, trying his best to be stoical. Lovely people! They inserted two other words into my head: if only!

Laura is okay, slept most of the night and her temperature now normal.

Brutal doctors, heartless, misguided, unbalanced, stupid and unimaginative doctors, crooks too, I have come across them all; but they were exceptions. Most doctors have the nous to realise, they are trained to realise, that they have chosen to peddle strange merchandise, one as desirable and popular as the other is unpopular, namely life and death. They are dealing repeatedly, often on a daily basis for years on end, more often than soldiers and much more often than civilians, with the ultimate human predicament. They can be successful, but in the end are bound to fail, for death is incurable. Their work can patch up, prolong, postpone, and be brilliant and idealistic; but it can also be seen as quackery, a tissue of lies, disillusioning, disappointing, futile and heart-breaking. To be too logical is not good doctoring. To be too empathetic and sympathetic ditto. The emotional content of medical practice is serious stuff. Nevertheless I find my work addictive.

Two nights ago I was at the A & E at St Anne's Hospital in Tinbury. I had done that duty in London; but there we had more staff around, including porters. And I think I only did it on week-nights; I was in Tinbury on Friday, pay day. The real trouble began at about eleven and subsided at about three the next morning. By then we had one lost eye, two or three broken arms, a broken leg, a broken pelvis and a broken neck – that is a list of the major casualties amongst members of the public, and does not include haemorrhages, cuts and bruises, hysteria, drunken incontinence and vomiting. Amongst the hospital staff and the police personnel trying to cope with the mob, there was a nurse with broken fingers, another with a black eye, others badly bruised, a porter concussed, a policeman hacked on the shin, another knocked out, a third with an injured knee, a fourth with a back problem, and I was hit on the jaw and the ear, spat at, sicked over, kicked and cursed. Cool Britannia! This is our 'culture'. This is the handiwork of our politicians and trend-setters. Are people worth curing?

I was not fit for work on the Saturday and Sunday because of the above, and took Ma to Matins at St Peter's Church. She likes it there not only because of the old stained glass, but also because gallant Parson Wetherby has resisted

34

the abominable New English Bible and stuck to the poetry of the King James Version. I am not very faithful C of E, and feel shifty in the House of God. I wish I was an RC, the priests of which church are empowered to grant absolution.

Ma ranted and raged against the generation that cannot wait to blot out reality with drink and drugs, and had hurt me. I agreed, but had to say that the favourite entertainment of humanity has always been escapism and varying degrees of release from reality. That is what art has to offer, ditto the pie-in-the-sky aspects of religions and Marxism.

Ma is planning to spend Christmas with the Proctors in Norfolk. Jane has invited her, and Ma looks forward to seeing her daughter and grandchildren again – she has not seen them for nearly eighteen months. She would like me to complete the family reunion. No, no, not for me, I am not ready for days of exposure to a happy family. I promised to put Ma on the right train and meet the train that brings her home to Maeswell.

The courtship of parents amazes their children. Ma amazed me by relating that she had only begun to love Father a year or two after they were married. In the hospital in Norwich where they worked and met, she did not take to him, she thought he was just another of the young doctors trying it on with her. Gradually he had worn her down and forced her to change no to yes. Why? Because he was so kind. Was she not taking a big risk to marry someone she was not in love with? Yes, but … 'He was steady, and patient when I flirted around, and women are born to be adaptable, aren't they? – and persistence usually does win fair lady.' I checked that Father was loving her while she was not really loving him: 'Oh yes – and sometimes I felt smothered, which was ungrateful.' How had she known when love hit her? 'Probably when I noticed that I was worrying about him as much as he worried about me. I wanted him to be happy and well more than to be happy and well myself. Love's lovely, but a life sentence. I didn't know what it was until it was too late – young people rush in because they're ignorant, not necessarily fools. We had become a team, you see, with our home and two babies and our own medical practice, and it was not a big step for me to see that we were inseparable emotionally.' She summed up their marriage: 'Your father was clumsy and an awkward customer, but he was straight as a die, he exasperated and amused me for all our years together, and I believe I was luckier than I easily might have been.' Her ending was philosophical. 'We were separated when he died, but only in one sense, and the comfort is that I don't wish my life had been different.' Ma certainly was lucky.

NOTEBOOK TWO

Two misunderstandings: A Mr Deon Lucas kept an appointment with me. He was a new patient, fortyish, with shorn skull and heavy black moustache, wearing a T-shirt under a bomber jacket. His voice was high-pitched, his speech mannered, and he was a bit squirmy.

'Oh dear, where am I to begin?' he began.

He then said it was a very personal matter.

I asked for his address etc.

He brushed that aside, and said he had a more pertinent question to ask me: 'The point is, are you one of us or one of them?'

I replied that I was an impartial doctor ready to treat him.

'Well', he said huffily, 'you are single, aren't you? That makes you one of us.'

'Are you unwell, Mr Lucas?'

'No, but I am unsatisfied, Doctor Selaby – you have not satisfied me in any way – so I shall bid you good day.'

With that, he walked out of my consulting room.

Two days later another new patient, Mrs Carsloe, consulted me at six in the evening: a big black-haired woman, talking non-stop, in her thirties, wearing a dress and scarves. She slumped in the chair on the other side of my desk, and between giggles and tears told me her husband had deserted her. She hung her head, covering her face with her hands, then looked at me flirtatiously.

'How can I help you, Mrs Carsloe?'

'Pat to you,' she replied. 'I'm lonely, Doc.'

'There's no medication for loneliness.'

'You're wrong there, Doc.'

I realised she was under the influence of something and caught her drift.

I said: 'You should see Dr Fletcher, our lady doctor, Mrs Carsloe. I suggest you go and ask for an appointment with Dr Fletcher now.'

'You've given me nothing for my pain, Doc.'

'What pain?'

'Here.'

She patted her stomach.

'Dr Fletcher will examine you.'

'A female doctor's not my type,' she said, and jumping to her feet she raised her dress and revealed a daunting nakedness.

I pressed the alarm bell under my desk and told Mrs Carsloe to leave my room. Mr Peele came to my rescue, but not before the lady who was no lady shouted at me: 'You don't like women, that's your problem, Doc!'

The Journal of a Disappointed Man plucks at a nerve. It charts the disintegration of a youth afflicted with life-threatening disease – he died in his mid-twenties. It is perhaps too sad to read for pleasure, notwithstanding its literary merit. I am ashamed to own up to a trace of fellow-feeling for the title.

Mrs Symonds has not deprived me of her company. No week of these last months has passed without her bringing me an ailment or two or three. Today they were pins and needles in one foot, pain in the other hip, a suspected frozen shoulder, and indigestion.

'I'm sorry to be a wreck,' she said with a disarming smile. 'And I rattle with all the pills inside me.'

As usual she twisted me round her little finger. We doctors are all deformed by having been twisted round so many little fingers. I was also impaled on the horns of Mrs S's dilemma. If she happened to be as wretched as she said she was, and either fell more recognisably ill or expired, the NHS might be sued for neglect by her relations and I might become a political football. I offered her sympathy and tentatively a referral to a psychotherapist. She was quite keen to have an opportunity to talk about herself to a captive audience at great expense to the taxpayer, but wondered if she should have an examination of her innards. I suggested a colonoscopy and provided details of what it involved. She was unshaken. She is a masochist, and I must be one to continue as her doctor.

But I like Mrs S. I do not like Mrs Quinn, an unmarried mother of three from the Haven Estate, run-down council-housing inhabited by no-hopers. She is in her twenties, dirty, tooth missing, braless, and a wheedler. She had bitten me once before with her wheedling. Today it was her head and the unbearable pain that was not alleviated by any OTC painkiller: could she have something stronger? I urged her to stick to Paracetamol – I knew her game and was refusing to play. She demanded morphia. I gave her a prescription without explanation and shooed her out of my consulting room. At least the pills I prescribed are not lethal. I wonder if these drug addicts have any idea of how disgusting they are. Apparently they complain to dentists of acute toothache in order to get a shot of anaesthetic into their gums.

St John's Surgery is housed in a Georgian residence with gracious rooms on ground and first floors. The ground floor has been divided into Reception, Frank Cunningham's and my consulting rooms, nurses' practice rooms and a rest-room for medicos.

The doctors drift into the rest-room for refreshments and are sometimes all together there. Occasionally we discuss problems posed by our patients. Otherwise we arrange duty rosters and gossip.

One day Frank Cunningham unbent to ask me if I happened to be a devotee of the sport of kings. I replied no, but that I was intrigued by his interest in the sport.

An interesting conversation ensued.

Frank explained, as I remember: 'I think it

was formed by the contrast between my work with sick people and the health and strength of beautiful racehorses in the pink of condition. I'm not a gambler, but Penny enjoys losing an affordable fraction of family funds year on year without fail. Racing's our relaxation for different reasons. We'd be glad to take you to a race-meeting should the opportunity arise.'

Denis Woods was present when Frank was speaking in his kindly precise manner, and piped up to charge him with supporting the aristocratic principle.

Denis continued: 'Racing anyway on the flat is all about breeding and lineage, isn't that true, Frank? Perhaps you also like it for that reason – I do, in principle, although I don't go to race-meetings. It always amuses me to hear and read that the masses rush to Ascot and races everywhere on every day of the week, while the socialists and communists are doing their level best in the name of the "people" to polish off the toffs, pull down the old families, and preach that only they, no one else, are allowed to be more equal than others.'

Denis should have been a politician. But he might not have succeeded since he has too much common sense for that line of work. He is a thoroughgoing royalist and traditionalist. He produced a little list the other day, names on a card, which he aims to show to any republican who crosses his path. The list was of presidents and pseudo-sovereigns who have ruled nations in modern times, and he gave me a copy. Here are some of the alternatives for hereditary and constitutional kings and queens: Lenin, Stalin, Hitler, Mussolini, Chairman Mao, Pol Pot, General Amin and the other African despots, and the Middle-Eastern thieves and homicidal maniacs.

I have volunteered for the 10 am to 2 pm doctor-on-call duty on Christmas Day – not altruistically, but to have a reason to refuse possible invitations and not to have to celebrate publicly. I shall go to Early Service and eat and drink less.

There are still 'shopping days to Christmas', but I have already metaphorically wrapped my present for my colleagues. I am repaying their hospitality, and entertaining my new friends, by means of an office party. The 'Surgery Party' will be mine – I have booked and instructed caterers. The guest list will include wives, partners, children, pharmacists, and of course doctors, receptionists and Mr and Mrs Peele. The party will begin at six-thirty on Christmas Eve, after evening surgery, and finish at nine-thirty. There will be a buffet and wines, other liquid refreshments, and the 'venue' will be my consulting room and Frank's and the waiting-room – Frank and I will vacate our rooms early on.

The Poor Cottage has no central heating, and wind whistles through the space between the tiled exterior and the interior walls of lath and plaster. It is romantically ancient and historic, but I have no love to keep me warm.

42

*   *   *

Yesterday I paid Ma a compliment which she
was not altogether flattered by. I told her she
was good at growing old. The context of our
conversation was that Susan Ledbridge, a chorus
girl of yore, nowadays my patient, was attempting
to show the other old ladies at Silver Court that
she could still kick up her heels – do a chorus
girl's high kick – and had fallen flat on her back
and fractured her pelvis. Another patient of mine,
Mrs Marlbury, suffers from the overweening
ambitions of dotage: in her eightieth year she
booked herself into a package tour of the
Himalayas, the foothills thereof but the Himalayas
nonetheless. Result – Mrs Marlbury fell down,
was concussed, broke a leg and ribs, and had to
be carried for five miles over rough terrain by
Sherpas – she was in a blanket slung from a
pole. She spent six weeks in a Nepalese hospital,
and is now home, a very much poorer but
apparently not a wiser woman. Ma, conversely,
in her widowhood, moved into a sheltered one-
bed flat in the warmer south of England, wears
clothes with pockets instead of carrying a bag,
gave up driving ages ago, and has savings which,
she says, would cover the expense of a nursing
home if she had to end her days in one. I
thanked her for not worrying her children unduly.

A good example of how bad old age can be
stumbled into my consulting room yesterday. He
is a pseudo-gent called Tower, and was a new

43

patient. He refused assistance and barked at my suggestion that he should have elbow crutches or at least a stick. He is in his eighties – would not give his exact age – had forgotten his address – and had clearly had a stroke, one side of his mouth was paralysed.

He wanted to know what was wrong with him: 'What's up? You tell me that!'

I did so.

'That's wrong for a start,' he said. 'I'm fit, except my legs aren't what they were. I'm A1 apart from the legs and a headache.'

I asked: 'What medication do you take, Mr Turner?'

'No pills, if that's your drift.'

'You'll have to take some in order to avoid a second more serious stroke.'

'I haven't had no stroke and I'm not having another – and I'm not here for pills.'

'You should take an aspirin a day.'

'No – they make my belly ache.'

'And I could give you another pill to ease the headache.'

'No – I'm not taking pills. You think again, doctor, and tell me what's up.'

'You're old, Mr Tower, and your arteries and veins are hardening. You'll have a stroke or a heart attack next.'

'You're as bad as my daughter.'

'You have a daughter?'

'Not your business.'

'Does she live with you?'

'Mind your questions! Somebody has to look

after me. My old woman died twenty-five years past. The girl had to see to her mother first. That's the rule round here, that's what daughters are for.'

'It sounds as if your daughter would be fifty or sixty, and has looked after her parents for half a century or so.'

'Could be. Why not? I've kept a roof over her head. And she shouldn't speak to me like she does, and no more should you. Question is, can you do any good or not?'

'Answer is, sorry, Mr Tower. For your daughter's sake I'm not giving you a prescription. I don't expect to see you again. Goodbye.'

'What you getting at? I don't like your tone. Thank you for nothing.'

He dragged himself up and lurched out of my room, and surely returned home to torture his daughter – but not for long, perhaps thanks to me.

Missed church on the last two Sundays and regret it – duty took precedence. I would like to think the faith I had in my boyhood can be recovered. Science led me in an agnostic or even atheist direction; but now I see that science can only doubt and reject belief – it cannot consistently or logically scoff at or spurn faith, since science itself, its discoveries, its conclusions jumped at, are very often founded on faith. Remember medical science's changes of mind about the treatment of TB and mental illness, remember astronomy! Where are the fever hospitals of yesteryear, the laudanum for sale OTC, the Big Bang that was more believable than the Book of Genesis? Where are the Valerian drops, the bleeding cups and the leeches? Scientists used to subject mental patients to five or ten years of weekly sessions of psychoanalysis not necessarily because they were crooks, but because they had faith – faith that brushed aside the useless and perilous realities of life on the couch, and the waste of time as well as money.

The disappointment inherent in 'getting ideas' is that you are almost bound to find out someone 'got' your idea before you did. My 'ideas' these days boil down to truisms and platitudes: but so be it. Faith seems to me to rank in importance not far below air and water – you can hardly carry on without it. And you can choose to have faith in science or in music, in anything or maybe, unwisely, in anybody – or in religion. My faith aged twelve was mainly acceptance of the choice made by my parents and teachers. My stirrings of faithful feelings now are in response to experience.

Father told me this story. He was working in a hospital in London for part of the Second World War. In an air raid during the Blitz he and other medical staff had to take shelter in a passage on the ground floor – it was not a particularly safe place to sit, but they obeyed instructions and were sitting there, ten or twelve of them. They were used to bombing raids, they were dealing with the casualties, they joked about bombs, were a hard-boiled team, and probably

46

brave to boot. The raid in question was vicious and the bombs began to fall uncomfortably close. Incendiary bombs fell in 'sticks' or 'sequences', and Father and the others suddenly heard such bombs exploding on the road outside the hospital, one after the other, nearer and nearer. And a doctor called Robbins dropped on to his knees on the floor and began to pray aloud, 'Save me, God, help me, God, please, God!' Father said that Robbins' action was more alarming than the Germans. There was no direct hit on the hospital – the bombs had left their craters in the roadway. I asked Father what he made of the episode and he replied: 'Robbins wasn't a coward, and he hadn't been religious. He was a good doctor and a scientist, but in an emergency he prayed.'

I sympathise with Robbins. When the chips are down, faith is better than none. Faith in God is chosen when people lose faith in people.

I met a woman in tears by my cottage. She had emerged from the graveyard of my church, and was hurrying to where her car was parked. I recognised Heather, the companion or concubine of Tucker Bee, and guessed that he had died and she had been at his funeral. I asked her in and gave her a cup of coffee with a dash of brandy. Tucker had died in hospital, she told me. I offered a few comfortable words, but said the wrong thing. She was furious, not sad. He had left her a pittance, not the house, and most of his money was divided between remote nephews and a football club. Why do so many women fall for rotters? Why do men marry viragos, for that matter? Heather has a thatch of colourless hair you could not easily run a comb through, her face is colourless too, and lined and creased. She had served him for ages, and did not know why she had bothered to be at his funeral.

Everything is our own fault.

Mrs Peele has invited me to tea on Christmas Day. I accepted gratefully.

The old widower who asked me for Viagra has died in the bed of another old boy's wife. A scandal and a fiasco, no doubt to be repeated *ad nauseam* thanks to erectile aids for men and the contraceptive pill for women.

Free condoms were offered by the government to the Headmaster of a Catholic public school – 'public' meaning 'private' in this connection in good old muddle-headed England. The headmaster said no. The bureaucrat was not amused and demanded an explanation. The headmaster replied: 'We teach a form of contraception that offers the safest sex. It's called abstention.'

A good doctor ought not to be too susceptible to the emotions of patients or the charms of the opposite sex. Women are apt to be naughty with their doctors. They make appointments for non-medical reasons, discuss their sex-lives in an inflammatory manner, strip off before they are asked to, complain of lumps in order to be palpated, and linger in meaningful positions. A few declare their interest point blank, and occasionally a woman pursues her doctor out of office hours, threatens and attempts to blackmail him. He should be resistant and immune.

Is the above wishful thinking?

Iris made it easier for me to ignore red herrings in London.

As the Christmas Eve party looms up, I am reminded of the local red herring called Nicky.

I fear my party was a mistake. Father said that doctors, ideally, should steer clear of such events.

It is Boxing Day. A week has passed since I scribbled Father's advice that I ignored. Now I have some free time until the year turns. The party was no fun for me. I had omitted to include Bob Clutter, our nightwatchman, a shadowy figure I had only met a couple of times; Bob, invited on the morning of the party, told me that he and Mrs Clutter were deeply offended. Then the champagne lacked bubbles, the white wine was sour, the red rough on the palate, and the caterer's finger-food solid cholesterol; one or two of the guests lit cigarettes in our strictly smoke-free zone; and our pharmacist's boyfriend spilt red wine on the carpet of Frank Cunningham's consulting room. In the middle of the party a tipsy yob gate-crashed, seized a glass of wine from a tray being carried round and demanded in a loud voice, 'Where's the poison cupboard?' He was ejected by Mr Peele and Bob Clutter after a struggle.

Goodbyes were mixed blessings. Frank referred to our 'first ever cocktail party' at the Surgery, suggesting that it would be the last if he had any say in the matter. Penny Cunningham urged me to find a nice little wife to be my hostess. Denis and Alyson Woods were both under the influence, he said he would cut off the wrong leg if he had to do an amputation, and she prayed not to be breathalysed as she drove him and their children back to Deacon's Holding. Audrey Fletcher was doing her level best to control Andy's intake of alcohol, marshal their children, and be nice to everyone. Annie Miller's husband made a lavatorial joke, saying that he could not wait to provide a specimen. The receptionists headed off into the night tripping and giggling. Mrs Peele reminded me of tea on the next day.

What was particularly mixed about the blessing of the end of the party was that Nicky stayed behind. I have already confessed to awareness of her attractions. She has a big smile and a firm figure. She is twenty-five, unmarried but seems very knowing, is good with men as well as with female patients, and her manner is sympathetic with sauciness thrown in. We had never spoken much except on business – no conversation – I was careful not to converse; but we had communicated otherwise, by ocular means, by meetings and greetings, on her side sartorially and on mine by evasiveness. She wore civilian clothes at work, T-shirts and trousers, tight T-shirt, tighter trousers and no panty line.

Somebody should write a booklet entitled, *How to change men's minds.* More to the point, Nicky could. She wore a flimsy almost see-through dress, nothing to keep the cold out. She had half-pirouetted to show it and herself to me. 'Do you like it? . . . Why not, it's Christmas Eve . . .' She was beautified by make-up – feminists, forget your naturalistic rules and regulations if you should weaken so far as to want a man! Her eyes shone and twinkled with the aid of mascara, and her teeth were whiter because her cheeks were as rosy as blusher could make them. She was ever ready to help with the party chores, taking coats, pointing out the lavatory, and continually caught my eye in spite of my attempts to avoid hers. She was flirting, she had come out of the closet to declare her interest, she was on the warpath. Even when she helped to clear up the mess in Frank's consulting room, she scrubbed the carpet in such a way that it became a proposition, kneeling there and smiling at me over her shoulder.

She lent the caterers a hand as they packed their equipment. Then Bob the nightwatchman said he would check the upper floors and switch out lights. The time was eight-thirty-ish.

'What's next?' she asked me, laughing.

I laughed too, a bit breathlessly because of excitement, also uneasily, since I had no plan for the rest of the evening.

'What indeed?' I replied, indicating that the party after a working day had been tiring.

She approached me and put her hand on the lapels of my jacket.

'It's still early,' she said. 'And my flat's round the corner. Would you like to come back with me?'

'I don't know...'

'Come back with me, Joe.'

Verbally she was taking liberties. She had never before called me by my Christian name, let alone its abbreviation. Nurses are meant to be respectful to doctors.

'Thank you...'

I had twice not finished sentences.

'I could feed you.'

She laughed again, perhaps at the double meaning.

I bent down to kiss her because I was nonplussed. I intended to kiss her cheek – or thought that was my intention. I did not know quite what I wanted or was doing.

Her lips met mine. She closed the gap between us. Words failed me, but actions spoke volumes.

In time she broke away and, holding my hand and looking up at me with sensuously heavy-ridded eyes, murmured: 'Come with me.'

'I must fetch something from my room,' I said.

She let me go. I sat at my desk without turning on the light. I sat in the dark and saw a little more clearly. Remembrance was like cold water. I rejoined Nicky, who was waiting in the Waiting Room, and said I was sorry.

'It's no good – it wouldn't be good for either of us – I can't – forgive me.'

She had a sort of wrap round her shoulders. Her expression changed from happy to inquiring to disbelieving to sad. She plucked at her wrap, rearranging it to keep out the weather.

'What a pity!'

She smiled and added: 'Some Christmas Eve!' and then, 'Night, Joe.'

I stayed in the Surgery for a quarter of an hour – I was afraid she might be waiting in the street. At nine I was back in The Poor Cottage.

In the night, and afterwards, in the next days, the question that dogged me was: could I continue to practice in Maeswell?

On Christmas Day I spent the morning in my consulting room, had a couple of hours at home, and went along to the Peeles' at four-thirty. Their sitting-room is warm and cosy, as they are. A coal fire burned in the grate, the room was filled with souvenirs of people, places, holidays, his army records, their Christmas cards. I sat in a plush covered chair facing the fire, they sat in their habitual chairs on either side of it. Plates were passed round and then a cake-stand with jam sandwiches to start with and slices of Christmas cake to follow. The tea was strong and reviving. The Peeles could have given many people who thought themselves upper class a lesson in good manners and the art of hospitality. We discussed my party, my family, their family, the Royal Family, and the scandals of the town, the overweight mayor, and the disgraced publican who had vanished with the Christmas Club money – the sweet evergreen clichés. Mr Peele related that he and Mrs P had 'walked out' for eight years before they could afford to marry. They had been husband and wife for just on half a century, and never forgot to be thankful that they had survived the war. They had a son who was a chartered surveyor, married to a good girl and living in Tinbury, and a daughter married to a sailor and living 'down Plymouth way'. They had eight grandchildren and showed me the photographs. They helped me temporarily.

I worried about Nicky, too. Should I ring her, and encourage or upset her all over again, or not ring her and behave like a chauvinist cad? Saying sorry often makes matters worse, but I do say it inside.

Three more 'free' days – I only have to be on duty at the surgery for a couple of hours on one of them. The new year beckons and should inspire me to begin again. Instead, I retreat into the past.

In those dark moments in my consulting room I saw writing on the wall, and drew an odious comparison. I could not bear to let history repeat itself. I could not compound my error. Iris was a popular person, we all 'loved' her – she was an occasional member of our 'gang' of medical students. We were all working hard and recreated ourselves as a rule in a cheap Chinese restaurant where we ate long-drawn-out meals and drank gallons of beer. Female hangers-on joined in, girlfriends, mistresses – Iris seemed to me to belong in that pigeonhole; whether or not she slept with one or more of us, I never knew. She was four years older than me, a stocky but smart young businesswoman – she worked for a pharmaceutical company. She had blonde hair, cut short and smart, a rather bony face, a wide white smile, and warm hands and well-manicured fingernails. Her parents were divorced; her father lived with a woman in the South of France, her mother in the North of England; she had a sister, married with two children, in Ireland; and she was a broadminded Roman Catholic. I found these things out later on, at first she was just an agreeable acquaintance, someone I sometimes linked arms with in the street, when a crowd of us marched home after blow-outs of crispy aromatic duck and crispy noodles.

I had had my share of girls on pedestals. I adored them in theory, not practice. For me, becoming a young doctor in a hospital was almost exclusive of dalliance, I was so overworked and exhausted. At long last I was granted leave, which, by chance or Iris's good management, coincided with a conference in a hotel in the country paid for by the company that employed her. She was to be in attendance there. She said I might like to string along – I could relax while she was conferring – and she wangled accommodation for me. On the first of the two nights of our stay she scratched on the door of my single room when I was reading in bed. I opened the door and asked what was wrong. She laughed quietly with a finger to her lips, let go of the skirts of her dressing gown, and showed me she had no clothes on.

It is eleven o'clock on New Year's Eve. Ten minutes ago the telephone rang. When I lifted the receiver the caller rang off. Could it have been Iris? Could I have telepathically summoned her by writing the above? Oh God, not that! Or could it have been Nicky?

On the first working day of the new year I asked Nurse Annie for news of N. Annie said N had not been well over Christmas, but would be coming in to work tomorrow. She said it stiffly. Annie, unlike everyone else, had not thanked me for the party. She must blame me.

I have seen N. She was at the Surgery, looking much the same apart from shadows under her eyes – no make-up, of course. We met on the stairs. I said, 'How are you?' She replied, 'Alive,' and then, 'Don't worry.' And she winked at me and laughed.

This evening, contrarily, I feel more depressed, and not up to writing the sequel to the true romance of Iris and Joe.

A disagreement at the Surgery, not quite a row, unpleasant nonetheless, although it does take my mind off my trespasses. The story is that a mother brought in her daughter, a girl in her late teens, and demanded an emergency appointment with a doctor. They were called Spade, Mrs Spade and May Spade, and were rude and provocative. Dr Woods agreed to see them. May had stomach pains, and her stomach was distended. Denis, after a cursory examination, told Mrs Spade that the cause of the trouble could be wind, pregnancy, a twisted gut or a tumour. I could imagine Denis giving his opinion in his throwaway style. The effect on the Spades was dramatic. They had howling hysterics. Denis managed to pass them on to Audrey Fletcher, who always treats our female patients with problems in their private parts. Audrey ruled out pregnancy and wind, but again dropped the word tumour and referred May to a specialist who would be able to knock that suspicion on the head. The specialist duly obliged: May had a blockage, largely due to diet, but nothing worse. The relief of the Spades took an aggressive form. Mrs Spade returned to the Surgery with Mr Spade, a builder. They broadcast the news that May had fallen into a decline since being warned that she might have cancer – could not eat, sleep, leave her bedroom, was terrified, frightened to death, and it was all the two doctors' doing, Woods and Fletcher. They threatened legal action. Frank Cunningham was summoned to talk to them, but he brought them into my room – we explained? argued, apologised and offered prescriptions of tranquillisers for May. At last they departed. Frank summoned a meeting of his colleagues in our rest-room. He put Denis and Audrey in the picture, and said that he foresaw no danger from the laws of the land – the Spades would surely not obtain financial compensation from our Surgery, however asinine the lawyers; but he deplored the medical fashion for doctors sharing their thoughts with patients. I sided with Frank – I have always thought it cruel to tell people they might have a life-threatening disease before the diagnosis proves or disproves it. Denis and Audrey spoke up for the modern attitude to our fellows and its rallying cry, 'We're all in this together'. They argued that the doctoral etiquette of the 'No cause for alarm' variety was outdated, untrue, euphemistic and risky. It put more pressure on the doctor and less on the patient, was not fair, and invited legal challenge and costs. They were not apologetic. They were not at all sorry for May. I can write here that I believe they were at fault.

Ma exploded at least a squib under me yesterday. She said after much preamble that she was thinking of moving up to Norfolk to be nearer her grandchildren. She denied that I had failed her. I tried to be objective and unselfish.

Perhaps I should go to Norfolk, too – uneasy at the Surgery.

Another upsetting experience: Mrs Thorner had an appointment with me this morning. She is a young woman, a girl, a child bride, twenty years of age, first name Norah. I called her Mrs Thorner, and she said, 'No, please, Norah's my name, Norah, please, Doctor.' She was agitated, pale-faced, all blue eyes and long blonde hair with a fringe. She explained that she is Audrey's patient, but had come to me because Audrey is on holiday. She is pregnant – early days – and wondered if I could give her a tranquilliser or something. Why did she think she needed a tranquilliser? She burst into tears. She and her husband Billy were not sure about the baby, they kept on arguing for and against abortion, and it was driving them crazy. She was not alone in being unhappy, Billy was unhappy, and I was not happy. She sobbed out her story. They were too young, they had nice jobs and were saving to buy a house, she had to live with her parents meanwhile and Billy with his, and they had taken care not to be stupid, but something must have gone wrong – and oh dear, oh dear! She would love a baby, but not yet – a baby would be their ruination – but they could not bear to be unkind. What was she to do? Could she have something to calm her down and let her sleep at night without harming the baby? I offered her my shoulder to cry on, and she clung to me in the sweetest way. I wrote her a prescription and apologised for not knowing how to stop people being sad.

Comparisons crowd in. More and more tugging at my heartstrings – or do I mean nerves? I now see Iris in a new light, as the subject of one of these notes and another shot at autobiography. No time for more this evening.

I told Audrey after she returned from her holiday about Norah Thorner, and she told me that between then and now a grandparent had died and left the young couple enough money for a deposit on a mortgage for a house. Apparently they are more inclined to have the baby.

Iris was my mistress for eleven years – no, I will not fracture English grammar to satisfy partisan pressure groups, the illiterates in particular. No, I was her lover, she was not mine, she was my mistress, and exclusively, I believed. She is a lovely normal woman. She did not seduce me so much as educate me. She was more or less my everything, teacher, guide, partner, companion and friend, and she was charming, tolerant, vivacious, good-tempered, good-humoured. She had a gift for getting on with people, women included. It was marketable, her popularity and her competence were appreciated by her bosses, and she kept on rising through the ranks of her colleagues at work. I introduced her to my family. Father and Ma liked her so much that Jane took against her. She was flirtatious with Father and brought Ma samples of vitamin pills. She was more of a success with my friends when they realised she was mine – my friends might have hung back before that – somebody else might have been involved with her.

We never lived together, which suited us. I

had a flat near my hospital, she had one near her office. We were both workaholics, I suppose. We tired ourselves out and were usually in need of peace and sleep. We met at weekends, we were apt to cohabit then, and took our holidays together. At first, too, we snatched at extra helpings of love. I would go to her place in the middle of a night or vice versa – we had each other's keys. In due course, Ma scolded me for not marrying her, and Father shook his head over the permissive society. But she scolded me if I apologised for not marrying her, and put her hands over her ears if I talked of hypothetical children. She was not maternal, nor sentimental, nor pleased if I let her catch sight of the cloven hoof of possessiveness, and not in favour of our changing any of our arrangements: at least, that is what I understood her to be. Marriage and all the rest of it was the straw that would have broken both our backs. I was committed to striving to make sense of the out-dated idiocy of the NHS. The years of our thirties, Iris's and mine, slipped by pleasantly and satisfactorily, if in utilitarian style.

The surprise, shock, eruption, earthquake was her pregnancy.

Early spring, the season of snowdrops and infections.

Nicky is recuperating from our kisses quicker than me. She laughs and gets on with her work. When we meet in passages or on the stairs she

61

looks at me with conspiratorially lowered eyelids. I remind myself that she was as much at fault as I was. If I had accepted her invitation, we would have strayed into the territory where fatal accidents happen. But I should not blame her for raising the spectre of the last act of the Iris drama – she and Norah Thorner.

Got to church at last. The Lord's Prayer fits my bill. Prayer for my patients, one MND, two MS, for little C and the other eleven cancers, for all the people who are ill for one reason or another, and that my diagnoses will not be wrong, and mostly for forgiveness.

My response to our baby was utterly self-centred to start with. To write that we both knew how the crisis came about is bizarre considering she was a woman of a certain age and I am a doctor. I mean that we both knew when and why it happened. On a Sunday evening in the month of July we motored out of London to dine in a country pub that was reputed to serve good food. It did, the food was delicious, wine ditto, the weather was warm and balmy, and stars winked and twinkled in the deep blue heavens. The circumstances were designed by the mischievous fates for the pleasures of the flesh. When we left the pub one of us suggested that we might open the rear doors of my car – perhaps there was no verbal suggestion, we just tumbled into the back seat by common tacit consent. Afterwards, Iris returned to the pub to wash as best she could, and then I dropped her at her address so that she could use her douche and take other belated precautions. We had acted on impulse. We were aware of risk, but vaguely in my case, because of her customary preventive measures, and vaguely in hers inasmuch as she kept a business appointment on the Monday morning instead of going to a doctor. I must agree that I was irresponsible and should have known better; but my defence would be that my dealings with Iris were a kind of dream of sex, of relaxation, nothing so real or important as my life or death struggles in the hospital.

Her announcement was doubly volcanic: she was having our baby, and I had never been in love with her. When the soft-focus gauze was jerked up and away, our relationship was revealed with new and cruel clarity. The mix of my metaphors is descriptive of my state of mind. Perhaps the theatrical metaphor is the more accurate: the stage of our love was suddenly and starkly lit, the hiding places were illuminated, we were revealed in the altogether, and I suffered a great pang of revulsion. It was momentary. I did not know at once that it was also irreversible.

I behaved as well as I found possible. Iris made it easy for me not to pretend I was ecstatic. She too was distressed, and no doubt saw farther than me: women have a maddening talent for seeing farther into the future than their men. We did not have to do anything in a hurry, it was early days. That we should have carried on as if nothing much was different, or tried to, can only be explained by the pressure of our work and our self-supportive beliefs that her business and my career took precedence over everything else. We had no space in our lives for an intruder. She might have been weighing pros and cons, although she did not let me in on the process; I was true to my sex to the extent of subliminally leaving it to mother; when we met we giggled shamefacedly over our baby, and we procrastinated. Iris did not breathe a word about marriage. We were children of the age of permissiveness, and she probably sensed the change in me and that I would run a mile from being a husband.

I have not done us justice in the above. I do not deserve justice. And is it caddish to tell the unvarnished truth in a document that will not see the light of day? These notebooks already bear witness to my faults; Iris's, such as they were, jarred on mine increasingly. Her practical approach overruled feelings, her common sense was positively coarse. She had no patience with my attempts to honour my parents: although she was ready to charm them, she ignored her own, and once stated that parents were 'history'. She mocked my concern for patients: 'Leave your patients in the hospital,' she advised. She often called me a 'softie', 'not a man of the world', 'not streetwise'. In good moods she spoke well of my sensitivity; when she was in a hurry, or simply impatient, she complained of my 'bleeding heart'. She minded her business even less than I minded mine: she was long-winded about her problems in the office, her climb up the greasy pole, her ambition and frustration. The act of love tells the full love story. I know I am contrary and ungrateful to acknowledge that her lips were too thin for kisses, her foreplay was brusque, sensuality was not given a lot of room in the beds we lay on, and her recovery time set records. Nakedness meant nothing but being unclothed to her – she paraded her body without aphrodisiacal discretion or shyness, and cooled passion with the misplaced enthusiasm of a nudist. The strength of her physique was more workmanlike than womanly.

I write as if I were Casanova or Don Juan. Truthfully, I had just enough experience of the opposite sex to have formed by means of elimination an ideal, that vision of the loveliness of the unattainable she. Iris and I made love over and over again, in several senses we filled vacuums for each other; but I have not yet got over the trauma of realising that I meant more to her than she did to me, and our eleven years were a mistake, a waste, and had not prepared me at any rate to pass the test that nature set us.

January has hurried by and we are halfway through February. Maeswell has not wiped the slate clean, after all. I cannot bear to look back at harsh things I have written about Iris, and shrink from writing the last act of our light comedy which gained a tragic dimension. Ma seems to have injected me with a yearning for greener grass.

A deeply embarrassing scene – Nicky marched into my consulting room after my evening spell of duty. She shut the door behind her ominously and sat down in my patients' chair. I had stood up, she asked me to sit down.

'Joe,' she said, 'why are you avoiding me?'

'Nicky,' I began, but she interrupted.

'You needn't be afraid of me – I'm not going to make trouble.'

'Nicky –' I tried again.

'I don't hold anything against you,' she said. 'You went off me, you ditched me – it happens – I wish you'd stop avoiding me, Joe – you're making my work difficult.'

I said I was sorry.

'That's the last thing I want to hear,' she batted back. 'Why can't you be natural with me? You give all your nursing requirements to Annie. I don't mind – I'm not complaining – I haven't lost my job yet – but how can I stay on at this rate?'

'It's not like that...'

She interrupted again.

'We used to be friends. Why does a kiss after a party make such a difference? It's ridiculous. I'd better go. You don't seem to know what I'm driving at.'

She looked tearful and stood up. I approached her round my desk.

'It's all right, we'll be all right,' I said.

I would have liked to put an arm round her shoulders, but restrained myself.

'Will it, Joe?'

'Yes – certainly – yes.'

'I shouldn't have come to see you.'

'Of course you should.'

'I'm not saying sorry – we can't say sorry to each other.'

'That's true.'

'Thanks, Joe.'

'Good night, Nicky.'

She laughed at me in a sceptical tone of voice, and walked out

Since then, thinking I may be the one not to stay on.

This is beside the point, but is comic relief and postpones the evil hour.

Mrs Symonds called in again. She had an agonising pain in the little toe of her right foot.

'What exactly do you mean by "agonising"?' I asked.

'Well, I had to take paracetamol in the night.'

'How many paracetamol tablets?'

'Only one, for goodness sake, Doctor – I'm not a drug addict.'

'And one common or garden tablet eased your agony?'

'Oh yes, I slept well after that.'

'Is it agony now?'

'Not quite so bad, but not good.'

'I advise you to take another paracetamol.'

'Aren't you going to give me a prescription?'

'No, Mrs Symonds. I believe your little toe will soon be hunky-dory.'

'Is that all?'

'Yes, but come back to me if you experience agony that isn't cured by paracetamol. You could come back for a scan or invasive surgery.'

'Thank you, I definitely will.'

But I was wrong to mock. Doctors cannot be sure of anything except the fact that nobody knows. A pain in a little finger has been identified as the only symptom of a cardiac infarction.

Ran into Norah and Billy Thorner in the street. They had decided not to abort their baby. They have done the right thing, counted the costs and are being brave.

I was not, I was appalled by the prospect of parenthood, and I think Iris was, too. But we did not immediately settle on the final solution of our problem. We hesitated, toyed with various ideas, even shook the kaleidoscope to produce rosy pictures. Strange to relate and hard to confess, we let the weeks pass. It was not intentional cruelty, it was a sort of kindness – we were being kind mainly to ourselves. And we had no time to discuss and possibly set in train the complete restructuring of our relationship, lives and careers. Maybe we each hoped the other would pull the trigger. Two occurrences squeezed the trigger without pulling it all the way. Five months into the pregnancy, Iris was offered a directorship of her company, the seat on its board she had striven for. Simultaneously a localised epidemic of legionnaires' disease forced me to work more than overtime – I and other doctors were battling night and day to prevent the spread of the disease and not to catch it ourselves. Iris did not like to worry me with her dilemma, and I was unavailable anyway, snatching meals and naps at the hospital. My intention was not to sidestep the issue, but I lost track of time. In what would have been the beginning of the twenty-first week of the pregnancy Iris came and found me in a hospital ward and said something about an appointment with her gynaecologist. I did not listen, or perhaps hear – I have no clear recollection of the snatch of conversation. I did not detain, let alone accompany her. I was treating a patient who was near death, no other doctor was available – but that is only an explanation of why I caved in. My patient died soon after Iris and I had spoken, my conscience smote me, I rushed towards the wing of the hospital where the gynaecology department is located, and outside the operating theatre I saw a male nurse with a stainless steel bowl in which, partially covered by a paper towel, lay the corpse of my daughter.

I was always uneasy about abortion. The Hippocratic Oath that doctors have to swear states: 'I will not give a woman a pessary to produce abortion.' On the other hand I was uneasy about women who should not have a baby for good reasons being unable to obtain an abortion legally. The argument is beyond me here. I do not agree with the free love merchants who have implied support for, if they did not advocate, free abortions on demand; nor with Tolstoy, who had all that premarital and marital sex and then told the world that love was not to be made except for the purpose of procreation. These notes are meant to be autobiographical. I collapsed at the sight of my dead child. I collapsed in the corridor, was attended to by nurses, and taken to lie flat on a bed in a Recovery Room. I 'recovered' there from what I had colluded in doing – that is, I was able to seek Iris out in a ward and sit with her. She was not tearful. She was relieved that a stupid mistake had been corrected. She was tired and I was silent. Before long I was allowed to drive her back to her flat. She had food stored there, she said she had everything she wanted and just wanted not to make any effort, to sleep through the weekend, and get back to work in the week ahead. We parted without any meaningful communication.

It took place some days later.

Even on pages that will never be read I must draw attention to my consciousness of being in a glass house, and assert that I am not going to throw stones. No blame game! Abortion is a controversy, a difference of opinion, often a necessity, never a laughing matter, always a sorrow.

I was with Iris in her flat on a Saturday evening. We had not met since I drove her home from the hospital, and scarcely spoken on the telephone. Her flat is high up in a modern office-

and-residential building. It has a balcony, great views, and is furnished in the minimalist style – almost empty, clinically tidy, cheerless and uncomfortable. You must be materialistic to live in such surroundings; but once I thought minimalism was smart. Iris welcomed me. She said she was fine, and that I looked worn out. She insisted on giving me a glass of red wine – 'It's the antidote to legionnaires' disease.' At this point she had apparently not noticed my state of mind.

'There's something I have to tell you,' I began.

'What's wrong? You're not ill, are you?'

'I need time by myself.'

'What do you mean?'

'I need to get away.'

'For a holiday?'

'To be by myself.'

'Without me?'

'Something happened, and...'

'Go on.'

'The baby happened, or, rather, didn't happen.'

'Are you backtracking on the abortion?'

'I raised no objections to it, and I'm not objecting now. But I have regrets, I do have regrets, and I can't shrug them off, and I need time to sort myself out.'

'You're deserting me.'

'Oh Iris!'

'Because I had the abortion – which you wanted but hadn't the guts to say so – and now you're sliding out – thanks a lot, honeybunch!'

'I saw our daughter.'

'What?'

'Don't force me to say any more.'

'Our daughter! It was an abortion. You liked doing what you did to make "our daughter". You owe me for setting you free from "our daughter". She's not the only thing that's going down the drain. I've given you eleven years of my life, and you never even offered me an engagement ring, not to mention a gold band.'

'Well – we live and learn.'

'You're not entitled to have more regrets than me. What am I expected to do?'

'You've always done what you wanted, Iris. You'll be a good company director.'

'What about you?'

'I'll carry on doctoring somewhere else, not in London.'

'Alone?'

'Yes. There's no third party. There's no party, if it comes to that.'

'I can't say I hate you, although I suppose I should.'

'You're not good at hating.'

'Or loving? Don't answer that question, Joe.'

Our conversation continued – no real row, no passion – typical of our love affair. She drank more red wine, and eventually said she had been hoping to have a nice dinner out with me. I offered her the dinner – we adjourned to the restaurant we had often patronised within walking distance of her flat. We talked of old times. She was hungry, but I had a brief attack of nausea during the meal. After I had walked her home, in the entrance to the building, she said she was not fit for copulation but was willing to try to give satisfaction if I was interested in one more for the road. I declined.

In the ensuing days my remembrance of my dead child kept on recalling me to the reality that had seemed to pass Iris by. I spent my odd half-hours off at the hospital in the chapel attached to the building. Grieving people came in to cry and pray. I benefited inasmuch as I realised I was more a religious than a scientific person.

Inevitably, when I came to live in Maeswell, Ma spoke of Iris. I told her we had split up, and she bemoaned the fact then and later. She said Iris would have been a nice wife for me – such a clever capable girl. She would have liked me to marry Iris and have children, grandchildren for her, in particular a grand-daughter – Jane's daughter Peggy was too rough and countrified. I told her that I had ceased to love Iris, and we had parted without acrimony. She scolded me with the oracular opinion of senior citizenship: 'Love's no excuse.'

A month has elapsed since I unburdened myself, and now it is more than a year after the events that changed the direction of my life. Iris has not bothered me – I no longer dread the telephone and the postman. I do not under-estimate all that I have to be grateful for. Wounds heal, although amputations can go on hurting: I still have pain in the space of my heart that was reserved for my daughter. I would love to love somebody else, but no such luck. Nicky, when I indicated that a few kisses were enough, minded more than Iris did when I indicated that I was bowing out after eleven years. Loves seem to have their different 'display until' and 'use by' dates.

Iris may have been as sick of me as I was of her. We were conveniences for each other. Her dragging matrimony into the argument amazed me. I was reminded of that girl we knew in Suffolk, a rebel who ran off with pseudo-gypsies, lived like a tramp, then got engaged to a childhood friend and hurried to Harrods to buy her trousseau and hand in her wedding present list. Iris had pretended that for her marriage, not rapine and pillage, was the fate worse than death.

Writing Iris 'out of my system' has had the desired effect, but the effect is double-edged. I have finally done the job I was waiting to do, brought down the final curtain, but now I walk home to The Poor Cottage more alone than ever.

I would have liked to call my daughter Rose.

Autumn is coming in, winds blow leaves off the trees, earth turns into mud, the days grow shorter, and I have decided to renounce self-pity. Life in Maeswell is not positively bad. My work is interesting. My colleagues are friendly, and Nicky and I have become platonic since she has 'gone out' with the man who delivers our pharmaceutical requirements. My cottage may be Poor but is my own, and I think I am healthy. At the same time I starve, my personal life is zero, a void, my work can feel like the treadmill. Ma thinks of leaving me in the lurch, and I never see any sign of a rainbow. Restlessness gains the upper hand. I cannot moon about like this for ever. In a big hospital I would at least have more nurses to choose from.

I wonder if I shall buy another notebook. The two I have filled with notes now look like the autobiography of another disappointed man. They were meant to be the preface to the second, probably last, and conceivably better phase of my life, but turned into my farewell to Iris and a memorial to Rose. My future must not be allowed to become a wasteland in the eyes of the Almighty.

Mrs Roecliffe in my consulting room today.

PART TWO

NOTEBOOK THREE

I am still here.

A modern tragi-comedy, subject the NHS, main character Desmond Cochrane, Irish Englishman, a late-middle-aged drifter, drinker, punter, scrounger. He did jobs badly, sweeping pavements, for instance, and earned his actual living by milking the Welfare State. He used to be Denis Woods' patient, but Denis refused to sign any more sick notes, so Desmond told his hard line stories to Dr Austen of the other practice in Maeswell. Dr Austen was apparently a dear old fellow, nicknamed Jane by all and sundry and reputed to be gullible. He was persuaded that Desmond had something radically wrong with an ankle, which shot out in a weird way and was laughed at by schoolchildren, and referred him to Mr Stonebridge, the orthopaedic surgeon at St Anne's Hospital. Nothing happened for getting on for a year, during which Dr Austen retired to his villa in Malta. Desmond complained of the delay, but was told that Mr Stonebridge had more important cases to see to than a funny ankle. At last Desmond was summoned to St Anne's. He arrived with a plastic water bottle in hand – it contained vodka – and in the hours he had to wait got drunk. A nurse summoned him eventually, ushered him into a cubicle, told him to undress, gave him the garb for patients having operations, and in due course returned to look at his ankles. Both were dirty, and discoloured due to bad circulation: she was under the impression that he was in for amputation, some of his records had been mislaid, and she had to ask him which ankle she should mark with the blue pencil. He was too drunk to tell her clearly, and she said, 'This one, or that one?' he mumbled, 'Right, my dear,' and she marked the right ankle. A porter arrived, pushed him in a wheelchair into an anteroom, an anaesthetist gave him an injection, and Mr Stonebridge cut off the wrong foot. It was a scandal, blown up by journalists and politicians, blubbed about by do-gooders, and landed Mr Stonebridge in court. The hospital's defence was Dr Austen's retirement, Desmond's drunkenness, NHS bureaucracy and a computer fault. The taxpayer had to fork out a vast sum of money to compensate Desmond, who spent it quickly on slow horses, but was content to have rendered himself eligible for counselling, Invalidity Benefit, meals on wheels, home help, and regular visits by a trained nurse, a vicar and assorted ladies bountiful.

Mrs Roecliffe brought her daughter Melanie to see me. Melanie is eight and asthmatic, her mother beautiful.

Father forecast the fate of the NHS. He wrote to tell me why it was heading for trouble – I have the letter still. Here are his reasons: medical science would make advances that ill people would demand and the state could not supply free of charge; more people would live longer and fill too many hospital beds; people are easily over-indulged and spoilt, and spoilt people turn on and curse the spoiler for not giving them more expensive gifts, such as instant medical attention, services, care and so on; and the NHS was always bound to become a political football, done down by politicians. Father had no faith in politicians, most of whom have no professional qualifications.

The Roecliffe family has recently come to live down here, in a house called Wisteria Lodge, near the village of Taylton.

By way of contrast to Mrs Roecliffe, and somewhat ironically for me, Mrs Petty was back with the same complaint, yet another addition to her family. She is a cockney, forty-nine, her partner a road-worker, already mother of seven, heavily built, no oil painting, opinionated, humorous, and probably a diamond of the rough type. I scolded her for not taking the pill. She said she had no time to take pills. Another of her remarks would be of interest to sociology: 'He will get at me while I'm cooking the dinner.' Yet another summed up sex for lots of women: 'I'd like to put it on the windowsill and pull the window down hard.'

*   *   *

GPs are a repository for secrets, GPs have replaced churchmen. The generalisation that explains the inherent risks of heterosexuality is that sex for men is a miracle of mechanics, whereas sex for women is child's play, as easy as falling off a log. Religions and codes of behaviour aim to curb the activities of women and give a man some assurance that his mate's children are his own. I think, I prefer to think, that all societies respect fidelity, self-control, restraint, and I know that faithfulness is enforced by some. Love and sex are twins, but love that cannot exclude promiscuity is not up to much. I still have a pedestal ready for somebody to stand on. Have I found her?

A paradox: the more we are permissive the less sexy we are. Not immorality but morality is the aphrodisiac. I write as a doctor in practice, not a puritan or a prude. I have enough women patients to make me suspect that love in a cold climate is not so hot as advertisements, films, the pornographers and the sexologists suggest. Satyrs propose and nymphos are willing, rapists do their dirty work and sodomites wound one another, but I get the message that the British bedroom is mostly slept in.

A male baboon, as if to comment on the above, serves female baboons in season while he looks around with a bored expression on his face and seems to yawn.

*   *   *

Shortly before I started to write in this notebook I saw change and decay everywhere and wondered how and where to escape from all the decadence: different now.

Melanie returned, thanks be! Her asthma is responding to treatment, but she is a shy and nervous little girl and might suffer a recurrence. She has large bright blue eyes. Her mother has grey eyes, quiet eyes.

Mrs Roecliffe startled me by saying her husband wanted a second opinion. I was doubly downcast. She said apologetically that her husband had heard of a London doctor who specialised in asthma in children. I said I quite understood and would forward my record of Melanie's case to the London doctor – it is the policy of my profession to co-operate with requests for second opinions; but my face must have fallen, for she said she hoped Melanie and her younger child, Tom, could be my patients on a permanent basis. The appointment lasted for less than ten minutes.

I hesitate to write down an absurdity yet cannot stop myself. At the age of forty-one I may have experienced the phenomenon of true love, potential love, theoretical love, love adulterous, immoral, unreciprocated, and obviously hopeless, at first sight. What it really is or was, scientifically, analytically, I cannot explain; but it happened when Mrs Roecliffe first appeared in my consulting room. It was unilateral for sure, it is almost certain to be another mistake – there is a father of the two children knocking about. I have become a 'don't know' late in life – I not only do not know a lot, as I had imagined I did, I know nothing – her Christian name, whether or not her first name is Christian, nothing to reassure me. How could I have changed in the blink of an eye from a despondent realist, a cautious practical man, into a certifiable romantic? There it is – the most hackneyed of clichés now apply – love is folly, love is blind, is brainless, reckless, incompatible with fear, and probably star-crossed My prudent persona is horrified. What does she look like? Love casts its own light on the beloved. She is tall, slim, has dignity, has grace, has those illogically 'quiet' grey eyes, smiles more sweetly than other women. I could continue, but have to break off, not least to laugh at myself.

I should delete the above. No doubt I will have reason to do so one sad day. Meanwhile I should note down the side-effects of Mrs Roecliffe. I could not leave Maeswell while she is at Taylton, and had better tell Ma, who might have thought of Norfolk because of thinking I was not settled here. I should tidy myself up, have my hair cut, buy a new shirt, clean my shoes; and blitz The Poor Cottage, burn old papers, and bury the dead flowers in its garden – I must prepare for the most unlikely event of a visit. I would be wise to come out of my shell, revise my reclusive ideas, and seize any opportunity to meet my neighbours – society is a dating agency first and foremost. Nicky Benning and I can now be Platonists together.

* * *

I veer between dreams and nightmares. The latter preponderate. The thought that strikes me when I consider both is that happy beginnings are commoner than happy endings. A hard-headed estimate of my chances is daunting – years of frustrated adoration, failure odds on, success reserved either for when I am too old to enjoy it or post-mortem. I remember books that tell me cautionary tales: Flaubert's *L'Education Sentimentale*, the story of unconsummated love, the heroine modelled on a woman the author met when he was fourteen years old, and Balzac's *Le Lys dans la Vallée*, again a story of unconsummated devotion. The road stretching ahead of me is paved with question marks that cause bumps and damage. I am trespassing. Is it madness, or masochism, after Iris?

With Ma yesterday, she again brought up the subject of Iris. I said I had never fallen in love with her. Ma said the equivalent of nonsense, and how could I claim such a thing after living with poor Iris for all those years?

'I never lived with her,' I replied. 'We met and parted by common consent when we felt like it. And she was never poor financially or emotionally – she let me go without a fuss, and I believe she's drawn a line under our affair as I have.'

'Is that right, Joe?'

'It's more right than a charade and pretence.

85

We haven't quarrelled over our bones of contention.'

'Was it ... was it only physical?'

'Maybe – but the physical side was never perfect for me – I'd call our affair friendly and lazy – we were preoccupied and didn't bother to disagree or look elsewhere.'

'I'm so sorry, Joe.'

'You needn't be.'

'But we thought it was love, your father and I always hoped you'd make a match of it, we couldn't understand your holding back.'

'Now I'll say sorry, Ma.'

'Your father and I wanted to be always in each other's pockets – that was how we described our feelings. We wanted to be close and have a family. Didn't anything like that come into your feelings for Iris?'

'No – yes – I thought so – and she too, I believe – but the fact is that love wasn't our top priority. Whatever our feelings were, they weren't strong enough to withstand strain.'

'I've never asked why you broke up. What sort of strain, Joe? Would you rather not tell me?'

'I don't know.'

'It was lovely for me when you came to Maeswell, but always a mystery.'

'We had a child.'

'Did you say...?'

'Yes – a girl – she was aborted.'

'Oh no!'

'I would have called her Rose.'

'Oh Joe!'

'Rose came between Iris and me, and Maeswell was to be the beginning of a new start. Iris wasn't more responsible for what happened than I was.'

'How did the abortion...? Perhaps I shouldn't ask...'

'It's all right, Ma. We dithered, we had other fish to fry – we were so busy and wrong-headed – and we took the decision late and in a hurry. And I couldn't go on living the life that had been the death of Rose.'

'I'm so sad for you, but thank you for telling me. Has being at Maeswell helped you?'

'I thought it would, I thought it did, then I thought it wasn't helping, and now I think it's given me a new lease – I shan't leave here for the foreseeable future, Ma. What about you?'

'I'm staying, too.'

'Not for my sake, not because of Rose? If you'd prefer to be in Norfolk, I wouldn't like to be stopping you.'

'No, Joe – the Proctors are rather too much for me – they're hard-up and frightfully hard-working, Jane and Neil are, and Tony and Peggy are young – I'd only be in their way.'

'We'll stick together, Ma.'

'I do hope so. Has anything else changed your mind?'

I had to laugh – she was as sharp as ever – Father always made a joke of her feminine intuition.

'Nothing to report yet, if ever,' I replied.

'Can I say good luck?!'

'Yes, Ma – thanks very much.'

I was thankful for the conversation as well as the luck. Ma will no longer imagine I abandoned Iris on a whim and left her broken-hearted. Later she spoke some words of wisdom that are worthy of note. She said: 'I was influenced to stay put in Maeswell by Ethel Harrop' – another resident in Silver Court. 'Ethel's a widow from London whose only son works near here – he's a solicitor, and married with children, he's called Timothy. Ethel fell over in her London house, broke her pelvis, lay on the floor for hours, and was discovered by her daily lady. Well, Timothy had a scare, and said it would be much better if his mother moved down to Maeswell, better for him because he could keep watch over her as he couldn't while she was miles away in London, and better for her because she would see more of her family, her grandchildren especially. Ethel followed Timothy's advice. The consequence is that she's lost all her London friends, locals and shop people and doctors, everyone she depended on, and has to try to make new friends at her age. She's very lonely and hardly ever sees Timothy or his wife or his children – they're all worn out by work and plans and exams and social engagements, and have no time for her although they do try to take her out to lunch on Sundays. She misses her old home, too, and can't settle in a two-roomed flatlet. Really, children shouldn't have those good intentions which make old folk miserable – the old folk would be happier to be lonely and die where they've always lived. We're all agreed about it in Silver Court. Anyway, I took the hint from Ethel. I moved to Maeswell just in time to adjust to it and settle down. Maeswell's my home, and to go back to East Anglia after all these years would be horrid, and far from helpful to you, Joe, because you'd worry and have to motor miles to check up on me. And I'd be a terrible bore to Jane, and the more so the older and dottier I became.'

First name, Mary – Mary Roecliffe. I consulted the grape vine: Sylvia in Reception told me that Mrs Roecliffe had rung for an appointment with Audrey Fletcher – that is, for a first appointment – but Audrey was on leave, and she agreed to let me attend to Melanie. Sylvia said Mrs Roecliffe had explained that she was acquainted with Audrey, and that Audrey had advised her to contact our practice if in need of medical help. I therefore detained Audrey in the rest-room as she scurried through it – she never rests – and extracted the information that Mary is married to Bruce Roecliffe and Bruce is a chum of her husband, Andy. Andy Fletcher is the rugger player, who struck me at the Fletchers' dinner party and again at the Christmas do as being on the chauvinist side. What would Bruce be like? Why did Mary marry him? But I know people should not be judged by their spouses.

We are being oppressed by the government. We

are bullied by clerks in Whitehall. We are casualties of the Welfare State and squirm under the heels of the do-gooders. We are now bedevilled by so much paperwork, forms and questionnaires, that we are considering hiring a retired accountant to cope with them on three afternoons a week at our own expense.

Bureaucracy and chaos, the two seem to go together. The other day a woman and a boy came into the surgery both bleeding and sobbing: she was Ellen Thursby, Frank Cunningham's patient, a teacher at the state school down the road, and he was her pupil, Tommy Iles. Apparently a bad boy called Glen had been expelled by Miss Thursby, but had forced an entry into her classroom, crashed a fist into the side of her face and possibly dislocated Tommy's arm, been arrested at last by policemen, escorted off the school's premises, and then let go. We had to send the wounded ones to St Anne's Hospital by taxi. Miss Thursby declared that she would never teach again, nobody could, in schools and a country without rules, discipline, order or law. We have three similar grievances. Audrey had to press her panic button the other day when two young people threatened to 'cut her up' for refusing to give them drugs; then a man zonked out on cannabis obtained an appointment with Frank in order to ask him how to slit somebody's throat – Frank had to press his button, too. Thirdly, Denis Woods was off work for a week after doing weekend night duty at St Anne's:

he was assaulted by a young drunk. As a result we are depressed to read that the liberals in and out of government are about to legalise 'soft' drugs and make alcohol available in retail outlets round the clock.

Robert Chimes wanted a bed for the night and I said nothing doing. I would have been pleased to see my dear old friend, but he is a barrister and would cross-question me. He met his wife Barbara at a children's party, married her, fathered a couple of children, and never looked to right or left – Fido should be his middle name. He nagged me for eleven years over Iris, compared me with bounders who sneak into gentlemen's clubs of which they are not paid-up members; and he would be equally disapproving of my having fallen for a woman whom I have met twice on other business, and is heavily married. Robert is down to earth to the point of being in it too deep to see the difference between a night with a beckoning star and a cloudy day with drizzle. I am not prepared to reveal myself full frontally to any satirical party.

Sorry to have missed Robert, and mortified to have caught an imaginary glimpse of my attachment to Mary Roecliffe through his eyes. He might have said I have retrogressed to the magic world of a premature second childhood. He might have suggested that I was like the lovers who pick on partners incapable of reciprocity for a variety of reasons and will never submit an embarrassing request for proof that they are beloved. Not so, not so! Something passed between Mary Roecliffe's eyes and mine when she followed Melanie into my consulting room, a message, if you like, a beginning, if you like, or the beginning of the end, as I would prefer to put it. The nothing that did happen, throughout the first consultation and the second, was much more dramatic and exciting than the loss of my virginity. And after all, there is magic, and there are miracles. I believe in the latter. How is life on earth and in the solar system explicable otherwise – nobody has explained it so far. Robert might scoff in spite of being a Christian, but which of us will have the last laugh?

Setting aside Mary Roecliffe for a moment, the farcical vicissitudes of Professor Lanskill have been something different – and a change is as good as a holiday. Philip Lanskill is old, eightyish, and eccentric, to put it mildly. He was a Professor of Eng.Lit. at some obscure University, is married to another superannuated academic, Una, and they live in a small house in Allende Terrace. Although they are both nearly bald, upstanding white fluff is their crowning glory, and their spectacles are like the bottoms of bottles. He has a deep voice, she squeaks, their home is thought to be unfit for human habitation, and they drive a vintage Hillman Minx. Not long ago they were due to drive to Tinbury, but the Minx was unco-operative, so the Professor went to crank the engine while Una remained in the driving seat.

The car was in the garage. He inserted the crank handle and managed to turn it. The car started, was in gear, crushed him against the back wall of the garage, his right leg in particular. He recovered eventually from this accident, returned home, and again decided to go for a drive in the Minx. He sat in the back seat and fastened the safety belt in case of an accident. When the Lanskills arrived at their destination, Philip caught a foot in the safety harness, fell out of the car and broke his good leg. At last he was sufficiently strong to rejoin Una in Allende Terrace. But he was frail, felt insecure, and tried to wire up certain locks and door handles in order to repel burglars. Inevitably he forgot which metal surfaces were connected to the electricity supply, gripped a door handle, received a tremendous shock, was badly burned and broke an arm. He is still alive. He is the patient of Denis Woods, who has refused to provide certification to the effect that he is fit to drive an invalid buggy.

My goodness! Audrey Fletcher has invited me to dinner this evening. She has asked both Roecliffes, but Bruce is unavailable and she wondered if I would be kind enough to step in.

I am dressed and just off, dreading a rude awakening.

Dread unnecessary, disappointments nil, sighs numerous, regrets futile.

It was a 'business' dinner for eight. I was the

last but one to arrive, Audrey was in the kitchen and called out to me. Andy greeted me without a handshake and told me the first name of the other guests, Alan and wife Tracy and Seb with partner Bubbles. Alan shook hands, Tracy said 'Hi!', Seb made a sort of bow and Bubbles said, 'Can I consult you?' Andy offered me a dry martini in a cocktail glass with a frosted rim: Bubbles explained, 'You drink the gin through the ice, isn't it loverly?' Alan was thickset with dark hair like fur, Seb was taller, bespectacled and with yellow hair reaching over the back of the collar of his shirt. Alan wore a grey suit, Seb a leather jerkin, and Andy a roll-necked jersey – Alan and Seb were tieless. Alan's Tracy was mutton dressed like lamb, Bubbles showed too much cleavage. The average age of the company was early forties. Audrey was having to cope with Kathy and Trevor, the Fletcher children, while she cooked.

The atmosphere was sticky. Andy is rough verging on aggressive, Alan was silent, Seb jokey, Tracy rather on her dignity, and Bubbles trying to live up to her nickname. We were to eat at a dinner table laid for eight in part of the open-plan living-room – the kitchen was behind a room-divider. The cocktails were strong, but the party spirit less so.

The doorbell rang and a moment or two later Andy led Mary Roecliffe into the room. Her appearance is like a blessing. She looks high class, discreet, open-minded, warm-hearted; reserved and friendly in my opinion.

94

She kissed or was kissed by the other people: were they linked by her husband? She bade me 'Good evening' – to my mind with a charming hint of intimacy or at least humour. She was offered and refused a martini. She hoped she was not late. She has rich dark brown hair and the prettiest smile. She is poised and holds herself well.

Audrey had taken the children up to bed and now joined us, not looking as if she had been working overtime. Andy made a revealing remark when she and I confronted each other: 'Quack quack!' She shook her head at his witticism and asked us to come and sit at the table.

I was placed between Bubbles and Mary – later in the evening we got on to Christian name terms. She had Andy on her other side. The food was prawn cocktails – already on the table; then chicken casserole – Andy called it *coq au vin* to amuse his cronies – which was dished out with vegetables in the kitchen; then chocolate mousse and cheese. The wine was white throughout.

Andy talked to Mary to start with. Bubbles talked to me. She is a nice person and would be nicer if she calmed down. She treated me to her medical history, which is quite long although she looked to me as fit as a flea. Eventually I was able to talk to Mary. So far as I can remember I said nothing of interest, perhaps the same applied to her, but I thought it all wonderful. She told me about Melanie and Tom, Wisteria Lodge, her enjoyment of being near Maeswell, and I told her that I lived in The Poor Cottage and my mother had a flat in Silver Court. Whether or not she was gripped by these exchanges is a moot point; but I felt we were at least at ease together. The one exception to our humdrum conversation was when I asked if she was a reader, if she liked reading books, and she replied with enthusiasm that she loved it. I mentioned that I was tackling Gogol's *Dead Souls,* and she said she had heard of that book but was sad to say she was ignorant of Russian literature.

We were interrupted – Audrey was trying to get general conversation going – I suspected she was making heavy weather of Alan and Seb – moreover she was hopping up and down to deal with the dinner and could not converse with anyone for long.

Audrey succeeded, but her victory was Pyrrhic – Andy and his cronies took over, talked shop, and nobody else got many words in. This happened towards the end of dinner, round about ten o'clock, and after our host had replenished glasses generously. The shop that was talked was money – the three men worked in financial services, Andy the stockbroker, Alan a banker, Seb sold life insurance, and I understood that Bruce Roecliffe was an independent playing the same sort of game. Words that were double Dutch to me, and effectively shut Mary up, were batted back and forth across the dining table: macro-economics, stagflation, bonds versus equities, dead cat bounces, toes in water, May and St Leger Day. I only raised my voice once, unfortunately to utter a howler. I requested a definition of a word often repeated, brick, which could not be a brick for building. They laughed at me. Seb said, 'Come on, Doc, you're supposed to be one of the makers of bricks,' which Andy and Alan thought funny. Audrey rushed to my rescue. She said: 'Take no notice, Joe – they don't know the names of the diseases you'll soon be treating them for – a brick is slang for a million pounds – which, as you and I are well aware, is not what we make.'

The party finished soon after ten. It was a weekday, people had babysitters to relieve, and early starts on the next day. On the way out I asked Mary: 'If I came across a Russian book I thought you'd like, might I send it to you?' She replied, 'Oh – thank you,' and we shook hands.

I could write a learned monograph on handshakes and kisses on cheeks. Some are good, some bad, judged by certain criteria. Mary knew that she attracted me, women know these things even before the men do. In the circumstances prevailing, I would give her handshake, the handshake of a faithful wife who is not averse to having made a conquest, ten out of ten.

It is two days later, and this morning Audrey and I met by chance on the stairs at the Surgery. I thanked her for the dinner party and said I had been going to write to her; she thanked me for turning out at such short notice, and told me not to bother to write. She said: 'I'm afraid it got a bit financial,' and I said it had been a most interesting evening. She asked: 'Did you fall for Mary?' I jumped, but managed an answer that was too affirmative: 'Absolutely, head over heels!' Audrey laughed and said, 'Well, she enjoyed sitting next to you.'

Love is not love unless it hides its face. I did not want to confide in Audrey, but regretted having missed my chance to ask her twenty questions about Mary Roecliffe. I was also suspicious of Audrey: what were the implications of her guessing that I would fall for Mary? Was she paying Mary a compliment, or casting aspersions? In short I was at sea – emotionally, nervously – since having been within kissing distance of my lady for two and a half hours. And I still am. My worst idea is that I have embroiled myself in a fantasy, and nothing will come of nothing; I have rebounded from Iris, and Mary belongs to a multi-millionaire and their issue.

Love at forty is not like love at twenty. It seems to me that the older you are the more impulsive and impatient, and the more difficulty you have in agreeing that the proprieties have to be observed.

A young man asked me to attend to a cut in his forehead. What was his story? He said the cut was a love-scar. I asked for more information, and he almost boasted that he was a bisexual. When I put on rubber gloves he called me a coward.

* * *

Frank Cunningham requested assistance this afternoon. I was at home, worrying about Mary, and in need of diversion. Frank drove me the seven or eight miles to the home of an old doctor, Dr Willy Monkton. I had heard the name, he had been a respected physician and was the friend of Frank and once upon a time his boss. Flora Monkton, the doctor's wife, was Frank's patient and had summoned him urgently: the reasons why were like scenes in a film. Burnside, where the Monktons had lived for half a century, was grim, grey and derelict. Creeper grew across the front door, windows were broken, paint peeled, and the verges of the driveway were virgin forest. We walked through weeds to a side door. Flora opened it – she was very old and hobbled, used a tall stalker's stick and spoke with a Scottish accent. She led us to a room that must have been a servants' hall in the palmy days. Dr Willy sat in a chair – a relic, hairless, toothless, and not all there. Flora asked us the following question: – what was to be done – her husband wanted to die and would be better dead, he was incontinent as well as insane, and she longed to take her own life? We drank tea and had no positive answer. There was no legal answer. Frank was depressed during our drive back to Maeswell. He chose to see the Monktons as living proofs of the decline and fall of our country. Dr Willy had volunteered for military service in the 1914 war and lost the sight of an eye. He had volunteered again in 1939 and contracted malaria that dogged him for years. He had bought War Loan, which was never repaid by government, and its capital value dwindled. His only child, a son, a soldier decorated for bravery, was killed. He had been burgled and mugged. He had sought medical treatment on the NHS and been infected with MRSA. Frank said that Dr Willy had been brought low by politics and taxation, bad medicine and lawlessness. Our drive took us through Taylton, near Wisteria Lodge, and my heart urged a far more optimistic line.

I wrote the above yesterday, and omitted a detail that affects me personally. Dr Willy Monkton married his patient – Frank Cunningham reminded me that it was unethical and said Willy was lucky not to have been struck off.

I am Mary's children's GP at present: is it unethical of me to be in love with their mother?

To church this morning. My religion commands me not to harbour the feelings I have for Mary. It may be splitting hairs, but I do not expect or plan to act on those feelings in the meanwhile, perhaps ever. The Lord's Prayer helped, as usual: I repeated 'Thy will be done'.

I seldom entered a church in the eleven years I was with Iris. She was agnostic or atheist, or pagan. I was not brainwashed by her lack of interest in religion, or influenced by her silly scepticism. The silver lining to the death of Rose was that I rediscovered my religion and derived most comfort from praying.

I would never again opt to be as uncomfortable as I subliminally was with Iris.

A girl of twenty-two called Cherry is the daughter of non-smokers, never smoked, has a non-smoking boyfriend, and has lung cancer. Ninety-year-old Bertha called me out because she was suffering pain in her foot, and in her cottage I was almost asphyxiated by the smell of cigarette smoke. She did not have gout, the foot had nothing radically wrong. I gave her a few painkillers, and in return she offered me a fag. Luck, and how to bear bad luck, is why religions were invented. In church I thought of the hostage I have given to fortune, and how risky my life has become.

I spent another night in the A & E at St Anne's Hospital. As a result I have a bruised calf of my left leg, where I was kicked by an intoxicated female teenage nitwit, and am exhausted, disgusted, depressed and the opposite of patriotic. Another doctor and I must have attended to at least a hundred drunkards and drug addicts between ten p.m. last night and seven this a.m., and we had four nurses to help us. The waste of our time and energy, and of everyone's taxes, is inexcusable: here, in my notebook, I refuse to play the game of hypocrisy and can write the unspeakable truth. The liberal excuses for drugging, binge drinking, yobbishness, hooligan-ism, violent behaviour and criminal activities are poverty, upbringing, schooling, unemployment, racism, class and frustration. Stale buns! So what's new? What is new is lack of discipline. The words that cannot be spoken, the ancient remedies for sicknesses of the state, are punishments that fit the crimes. Forgiveness of offenders is all very well, but the prevention of offences by fear is more protective of the innocent. At present there is no death penalty for murderers, even serial or most foul, no corporal punishment which would keep people out of prison, no meaningful manner of controlling children allowed, no end to benefits or state money paid to undeserving people, and in fact no rebuttal by the establishment of the popular belief that money grows on trees. I know the decadence of our country is attributable to deep political errors, Marxist-communism-socialism and the pipe-dream of 'Welfare'; but attempts should begin to be made to rectify them. These weekend blood-baths in Tinbury and elsewhere should be abolished chop-chop. And ultimate deterrents are no bad thing, as the politicians of countries with weapons of mass destruction keep on telling us.

I am not a reactionary. I just wish England would stop sinking deeper and deeper into the mire. I could say I was not 'political' if my employer, the Government, would stop entangling me in red tape.

Some talk of holidays in the rest-room today. I said I would not be taking a holiday for the foreseeable future. Frank Cunningham said, 'All work and no play...'; Audrey said, 'You should, you know,' and Denis said, 'Well, I'll be extending mine in that case.'

No more of the nourishing coincidences on which love feeds. Four weeks have passed since the Fletchers' dinner. I would not mind being a fly on an interior wall of Wisteria Lodge, but Bruce and possibly Mary herself might swat me. Hunger gnaws.

Sad case: I had to break the news to Maurice Branyard that he has cancer. He is fifty-something, husband, father, an accountant, who recently lost his job with a large London firm – there had been a whiff of scandal. Maurice became my patient a few months ago – he had lost weight as well as his job. His reaction to the news of his cancer was surprising. He told me he had begun life in an orphanage, his parents had abandoned him, had then spent a few years with a cruel foster mother, and aged four or five had got his foot off a snake and on to a ladder in the home of a good fostering family. Ever since, he said, it had been a struggle to rise in the world. He had embraced the politics of envy and become a socialist. He was also dogged by the fear of failure and slipping back to his beginnings. That was why he had tried to do still better and had done worse. Yes, he confessed, he was guilty of juggling a figure or two, not quite of cooking the books. Why, why had he needed to, why had he done it? Because, he answered himself, ambition is habit forming, he had wanted more than he already had, more money, status, respect, security. He wound up by saying that the temptation for 'self-made' persons to take a last step on the ladder is almost irresistible; and that because of his illness he now wanted less and less, nothing but life on any terms. Perhaps his case was not so sad as I had initially thought it.

I begin to think that Mary Roecliffe is my wild goose. I can foresee no future in flapping along after her.

A case with similarities: I was able to read the letter from the Oncology Department at St Anne's to Constance Plym, who cried out, 'Hurrah!' The letter was addressed to Frank Cunningham. He had summoned his patient, Mrs Plym, but was called out urgently and asked me to see her. She is middle-aged and motherly. She said to me: 'For five years I've waited for the "all clear", and regretted the chances I had not taken when I was younger. Such a mistake! Now I've been given something I don't deserve – nobody deserves it but I've been given it – a second chance – and by golly I won't let it slip through my fingers!'

Contrary or not, this is a draft of the letter I might write to Mary.
'It was a treat for me to sit next to you at the Fletchers', and to find out that you are a fellow-bookworm. I am sending you a book in hopes that you will enjoy it, *First Love* by Ivan

Turgenev. I also hope to have a chance of discussing it with you one day, but please don't feel obliged to read it. The book is a gift, and second-hand, as you can see – it cost me about 10p so far as I can remember.'

I shall try again, here is draft 2: 'At the Fletchers' you gave me permission to send you a book I thought you might like, and you also said you had not read many Russian books. So I enclose Turgenev's *First Love*, which in my opinion is lyrical and lovely, and surely very well translated by Isaiah Berlin. It's a gift – it cost me nothing – and a souvenir too. I hope Melanie is well, and you are too, and that we'll meet again before too long.'

A third draft, below, would tell the whole truth: 'I'm sending you *First Love* because it's good and because the title describes my feelings for you. I know I shouldn't declare myself to a married woman who has given me no encouragement, and who is unlikely to believe that she is the first love of a man of my age – but it's true. I was the "lover" of another woman for a long time, but that attachment cannot be compared with this one. Turgenev loved a woman who didn't return his love, he loved her all his life – is it my fate to suffer his experience? I don't care, and I do and will care, if you understand me. I aspire only to know you better, become your friend, be in your life – nothing more, realistically. Forgive me! Yours.'

* * *

I posted no book and no letter. I could not hint at, let alone explain, the significance of Turgenev's title in our circumstances, nor could she be expected to assume the role of Pauline Viardot-Garcia in a possible rerun of Turgenev's dramatic emotional biography. She would read *First Love*, if she read it, and simply follow the story of a boy in love with a girl and his discovery that the girl and his father were lovers. My drafts of letters remain in this notebook. But yesterday I remembered Mrs Plym and seized my chance for better or worse. My letter was as discreet as I could make it.

One consequence of waiting for a word from Wisteria Lodge is that I have given instructions to the girls in reception to assign Mrs Roecliffe to another doctor, Audrey preferably, or Frank or Denis. It was embarrassing – Bessie looked at me inquiringly. I could not supply reasons: which were that I remembered the Monktons, and Frank's comment that Doctor Willy might have been struck off for marrying his patient, Flora. Against my will, wishes, yearnings and hopes, common sense and the instinct of survival prevailed. If Mary should ever fall into my arms in my consulting room, if a magic wand should be waved for my benefit, I would not like to be disgraced professionally. That is a fact, the rest is fiction.

Nicky Benning is pregnant. She is going to marry her boyfriend, the pharmaceutical muscle-man, who delivers our drugs. He is called Nigel. Jokes have done their rounds in the practice: that Nigel proposed after spiking her drink with an anti-depressant. I congratulated her and she hugged me and said: 'He may not be a good fish but he's not bad' – a kind of compliment, I suppose.

Nicky is in her fourth month, and has told us she will be taking advantage of the new legislation affecting mothers: which means maternity leave and counting on getting her job back in due course. She has a friend, another qualified nurse, a delightful young woman who is able, willing and eager to take over. But the friend is youngish and recently married. We made excuses, we reduced her to tears, we angered Nicky, and instead engaged a grandmotherly nurse of fifty-five, who wishes to be known as Mrs Loft. Women of child-bearing age are no longer employable by small firms and probably by big ones; and I understand that men can also get paternity leave. The work-force will soon consist of children, old women and impotent men.

Mrs Pullen brought me a black eye this morning. The eye was hers, and it and the other one shed tears. She sobbed that Daphne, her daughter, little Daphne who was dim and pathetic, was the culprit. 'She hit me, Doctor, when I only said to her "Don't" – she reached up and hit me.' The worst of it was that Mrs Pullen had paid for Daphne to go to self-assertion classes.

Stunned!

I could not bring myself to write more than that word, stunned, yesterday. There were too many words, I was overwhelmed; I am calmer now, and with luck the hand that holds the pencil will not shake. Yesterday afternoon, about three-thirty, when I was at home between morning surgery, home visits and evening surgery, Bessie the receptionist rang me. Mrs Roecliffe had called in to return a book, Bessie said, and wondered if it would be convenient to drop it in at The Poor Cottage: yes, I said. Five minutes later she, Mary, knocked on my door. She was blushing, and no doubt I was. She had been bold although she was diffident. She was apologetic; but my welcome, however stammered out, should have convinced her that she had done no wrong in my eyes. She stepped into my house – my parlour, I could write, for it is my only sitting-room, but I would prefer not to suggest that I am a spider. She said she knew she ought not to be disturbing me – which is certainly what she had done, despite my assurance that she interrupted nothing. She said she wished just to have time to tell me how much she had enjoyed *First Love*. We sat on either side of my fireplace. She sat in the chair on the right, with the window behind her, and the light caught her hair as if to form a halo, and, when she moved, the side of her face and her eyes. She declined refreshments. She wore warm clothing, a skirt not trousers, and showed a well-turned ankle.

She said: 'I can't thank you enough for introducing me to Turgenev,' and I replied: 'I can't thank you enough for coming to see me and tell me that I'd chosen the right book for you.'

I did not tell her that I had meant the book to be a gift – I was benefiting from her regarding it as a loan – and the pleasant possibility crossed my mind that she was establishing an excuse for seeking my company.

We spoke of Ivan Turgenev. I referred to Pauline Viardot-Garcia, and she seemed to admire his lifelong devotion, almost dedication, to her – she did not find it foolish or odd. I mentioned other examples of voluntary enslavement, and the proven possibility of first love being the last for some men and some women. She agreed. Whether or not she took these exchanges in any way personally is not known. A strange thing had happened, our instant ability to talk to each other freely, in my case more freely than I talked to other people – stranger than it had been in my consulting room and at that dinner party. Conversationally, we crossed a frontier – we were in a world where words were precious and every sentence uttered by one was food for thought for the other. It was light stuff, feather-light, not ponderous at all, but she inclined her head as if to reflect on what had been said, and delivered her responses to me with excitement, as if they had just struck her.

We reverted to Turgenev and his book. She said he had conveyed the disappointment and disillusion of the boy to perfection. She sympathised with the pain of discovering that the object of love – the boy's love – was not so pure and good as he had imagined and believed. Was she convinced by Turgenev's description of love? Oh yes, she replied, but as if she meant to say, 'Of course!' What did she read? And when? I told her that I had done most of my reading before I was qualified and became an overworked doctor, but that recently I had again known the joy of losing myself in books. She said she had read *First Love* in one evening. She said she made time to escape into a book. What should she read next, she asked. I should have replied, *War and Peace*, but Tolstoy's book is long, if I lent her my copy she would not bring it back for weeks. I therefore said, 'Tolstoy's *Childhood, Boyhood and Youth* – it's at least as good as *First Love* – and you might like it even better.' She was dressed so nicely by my standards, informally, perhaps with the superior art that conceals art, and her complexion glowed in spite of her face being in shadow. She had a few freckles and wore a touch of lipstick.

'I should go,' she said.

'Please don't hurry,' I replied. 'I'm not busy.'

'But I've invaded your privacy.'

'It's the nicest sort of invasion.'

'The Poor Cottage doesn't really describe your home – it's so cosy and pretty.'

'Well – it doesn't feel poor any more – I might have been attracted by the name once upon a time.'

'How long have you lived here?'

'Getting on for a year.'

'I'm sorry you were ever poor.'

'I'm not now. Do you like living in Wisteria Lodge?'

'Oh yes. But…'

'But?'

'It's rather big, and I haven't got round to decorating it as I wish … but I know how lucky I am to have such a home.'

I said, 'I want to explain something,' and she looked at me nervously.

I continued: 'I'm sorry I can't be your doctor.'

'Oh, that.' She sounded relieved. Had she thought I would go too far too soon? 'Yes, they explained at St John's Surgery that you were fully booked up, but could fit in my children.'

'It has to be that way, regrettably. I would take care of you all if I could.'

She looked at me. We looked at each other. It was nothing much, yet it was more than I expected, had dared to hope, had experienced before. Her eyes rested on me quietly – the metaphor or paradox or whatever is intentional. She reached for her bag, a shoulder bag made of soft material. But she stayed put, and I detained her by striking a less alarming note.

'We haven't discussed the Fletchers' party.'

'No.'

'Are you and the Fletchers old friends?'

'My husband has business links with Andy. Audrey's a sweet person. She'll be my doctor.'

'I was a bit taken aback by Andy.'

'A lot of people are. I'm not a very social person.'

'Nor am I. I see too many people every day.'

'And I've added to the number.'

'That's different.'

'Thank you. I'll have to go.'

'Wait a tick – here's the Tolstoy book.'

She put it in her bag, we thanked each other, and we stood in the brighter light on the pavement.

She said: 'I went to a service of carols at Christmas in the church over there. I took my children, and I liked the vicar.'

'He's called Bill Wetherby.'

'You know him?'

'I go to Early Service when I can. He likes the good old-fashioned Communion Service.'

'You're lucky. At Taylton the vicar asks us to shake hands with one another, which isn't easy because there are so few of us and we're all over the church.'

We laughed. Her laugh was spontaneous and infectious, and she has pretty teeth.

We said goodbye, and as she walked away I re-entered the cottage, not wanting to spy on her rear view or overload our parting with sentiment.

Coming down to earth with a bump, I was called out by Mrs Symonds. Her symptoms were dramatic even by her standards: she claimed she had dripped with sweat for twenty-four hours and was convinced her end was nigh. It was warm weather for April and I opened her front door, which was unlocked as arranged. A blast of heat greeted me. I was in Mrs Symonds' sitting room. She was in an armchair by an electric fire showing three red bars, fully dressed in clothes that looked wintry. And I had noticed that a central heating radiator was on and that all the windows were double-glazed and closed.

'Oh, Doctor, this heat is killing me,' she had the nerve to wail.

My remedial impulse was to switch off the electric fire and the central heating, leave the front door open because I could not open any of the windows, remove my jacket and scold her.

'But it's only April, Doctor, and April's a treacherous month, and I was determined not to catch a chill on top of everything else.'

I fanned the front door to get air into the house.

'Oh, I will say that's better, Doctor – you have helped me and your visit wasn't in vain.'

I said: 'You might have killed yourself – it was like a greenhouse in here – didn't you know how hot the room was? And why are you wearing that thick-knit cardigan?'

'Oh, Doctor, don't you be crisp with me, please – I'm an invalid.'

'You can't be an invalid to have survived in a cauldron.'

'That's not kind of you, Doctor.'

'Oh well, good night, Mrs Symonds.'

'Aren't you going to take my pulse?'

'It's my own pulse that worries me – you've put my blood pressure up with your shenanigans.'

She laughed in her disarming way, and then I laughed, too.

The point of this anecdote is that it links up with another. In the coldest March morning, frosty, gale from Russia, a juggernaut driver called Darren marched into my consulting room in a T-shirt and jeans. He had a heavy cold and asked for an antibiotic.

'You're not wearing enough clothing,' I said. He said he never wore more.

'Don't you feel the cold?'

'Never,' he replied.

There is a class of persons who are born without thermostats.

Mary Roecliffe has established herself in my head. I think of her all the time, which is not to say second thoughts are excluded. Our ten minutes together in The Poor Cottage were for me rich beyond dreams of avarice, as a phrasemaker might say. I believe I enjoyed every emotion celebrated by lovers since Adam met Eve. But relations between Adam and Eve had a trace of ambiguity, and I had felt both at home with Mary and that I teetered on the edge of a cliff or a crevasse. I was safe and in danger. On reflection, realistically, probably, she called on me because she knew I loved her – I had made myself clear enough, anyway her intuition would have told her. She called on me because she needed support, reassurance, and knew I would supply it as best I could. I was not the only one to plot and plan, she asked for another book, she accepted the loan of one, she spoke of visiting my church. In short, she indicated that I figured in her future. We were in the same boat. But what future was that, and where were we drifting in our boat? I was in receipt of ominous hints in respect of her marriage, husband, even her child Melanie. I was not an accomplished adulterer, had not plumbed the adulterous depths with Iris, but I had treated patients who were and who had been; I had second-hand experience and book-learning. The fun of adultery is balanced by jealousy, the better the adultery the worse the frustration, and always the risk of becoming the adhesive that sticks a married pair together. Besides, it is often a mistake to marry your mistress or your lover. What was I walking into so blithely? Memories of Johnny-head-in-air haunted me. But then ... Then I realised ... Then it was too late. I have more ahead of me than to turn back to. I had committed myself and I renewed my commitment. Caring was reinforced by curiosity. And I am on the last page of this notebook.

NOTEBOOK FOUR

My mark for morality is nought. One of the worst sins is mine, and that it is so far not physical is neither here nor there. For consistency my mark is also nought. I have been dead against the permissive society, yet had sexual relations with a woman who was not my wife for eleven years. I sanctioned the abortion of my child, blamed the mother of the child for aborting it, and deserted her. I am a man of my time, and ashamed of myself. Yet I cannot be responsible for another sort of abortion, I cannot do it – God should not have invented love if He wished us not to fall in it. Mary may prove to be my penance.

Nothing has happened, nothing may ever happen.

I go for afternoon walks in the Forest of Ashes, extensive woodland owned by the National Trust in the Taylton area, and fantasise about a chance meeting and love consummated under the trees.

Supper with Ma in Silver Court. She cooked me scrambled eggs and crisp streaky bacon and toast on the electric rings in her kitchenette, and afterwards we had tinned black cherries and cream. When I said she knew the way to a man's heart, she replied that I ought to find a woman who would cook me regular meals.

'Do you mean a wife?' I asked.

'No, no.'

'I thought I heard an old record being played in the middle distance.'

'Well, she could be your wife if she cooked well enough.'

We had a laugh, and the subject changed.

'Gabriella's had a windfall,' she remarked.

'Who?'

'Gabriella Shelby – you must remember her – she's the unlikely spinster, and my friend at Silver Court. Well, she's made quite a bit of money.'

'How?'

'No, dear – nothing wrong with it – she gave some money to a man who works in the City and she got back twice as much.'

'Is he a stockbroker?'

'Something like that – a financial person – and she's bowled over by him – he's so charming as well as clever with money. He lives part of the time not far from here. He's called Bruce Roecliffe.'

Adultery Without Tears advises us to learn not to emote when we hear the name of the beloved's spouse bandied about.

* * *

To church at St Mary's, the early service, spoilt for me by entertaining irreligious hope that Mary might be there. In the good old days of attendance at church for all and sexual frustration, the joke was that 'Let us pray' should be spelt 'Let us prey'.

I had to laugh when I attended the death-bed of my patient Jimmy Lovell. He was an alcoholic and divulged some of the secrets of his fun and games in days gone by. He thanked God for vodka, which does not smell on the breath. He said he must have drunk a million bottles of brightly coloured fruit-flavoured liquid laced with vodka. He had hidden bottles of vodka in his compost heap and drunk it hot. He had sunk bottles in his lily pool and drunk it cold. He had not drunk everyman's drinks since he was a boy: his beers, stouts, wines were always reinforced by spirits, and his gin was mixed with vodka, his whisky with brandy, his brandy with those high-alcohol-content French liqueurs, and his liqueurs were an absolute witch's brew. He had held down jobs in farming, in racing stables, in building works – whatever sober men would not dare to do, he did because he was half seas over. The turning point for drunkards, he told me, is when they get their headaches because they are not drunk – their hangovers are caused by drinking water. Propping up a bar had meant happiness for him, and he had had a grand life, even if it was a 'short'.

On the way out of the Lovells' home I commiserated with his wife Minnie.

'He loved his bottle best,' she said, 'he never looked at another woman.

Common sense is blowing away groundless confidence. She has a charming husband, who can turn dross into gold: why should she bother with the inhabitant of The Poor Cottage?

I doubt even that this notebook will be filled. My opinions and observations are beside the point, and I cannot continue to put my preoccupations in writing when they seem to be pointless.

A coincidence of a most peculiar kind has occurred. I was on duty at St Anne's Hospital the night before last. It was a Saturday, getting on for midnight, the A and E was inundated with drunken idiots and casualties of fights, traffic accidents, street crime and genuine emergencies, and my professional patience was just about exhausted. A man and a woman joined the queue in the waiting area. They were well-dressed although informally, looked well-fed and well-to-do, and were exceptions both classwise and inasmuch as they were sober. He also attracted my attention by standing up instead of sitting down like the other people on the chairs provided. I kept on passing through this waiting area. Injuries etcetera were attended to in cubicles, there was a surgery for small operations and a pharmacy doled out medicines. Moving from one cubicle to another I was aware that the arrogant man, now seated, was holding his left hand in his right. The next thing was that somebody in one of the cubicles was kicking against a partition and raising his voice – Oxford accent – swearing that he was in pain and had hung about for too bloody long. Against my principles and the rules of the department, which were that troublemakers should not be allowed to jump the queue or receive preferential treatment, I responded. I drew back the curtain across the opening into the cubicle and told him to mind his language and behave – behave properly, that is. He had angry blue eyes and looked at me with daunting hostility. He had two dislocated fingers, the third and little fingers of his left hand. He thrust his hand in my direction and said, 'Can't you bloody well put my bloody fingers back where they belong?' I summoned a nurse, Stella, and then asked him, 'How were the fingers dislocated?' He replied: 'Mind your own bloody business!' When Stella joined us I explained in an undertone: 'This bloke wants his fingers seen to and I want you to record our conversation' – the senior staff at St Anne's A and E carry small recording machines.

I then said to him: 'The relocation of your fingers is possible, but painful. You are in a hurry evidently. I can do the job here and at once, or you can take your turn in the operating theatre and have a numbing injection or a whiff of pain-killing gas. It's your choice, sir.'

'You get the bloody thing done, so that I can go home.'

'You've chosen to have the two dislocated fingers of your left hand repositioned without anaesthetic, is that correct?'

'Yes and to hell with it!'

I mentioned the date and time, and he confirmed them. I sent Stella to collect the forms he had filled on admission. I then did the dirty work, causing him to squeal when I yanked the longer finger, to ask me to wait while he prepared himself for the little finger, and to squeal again and shed involuntary tears when I had to waggle it and push as well as pull.

He uttered a few more expletives of the fashionable kind, mopped his brow with his handkerchief and blew his nose, and remarked, 'What a performance!'

I replied: 'Everything you have said has been recorded, including your choice of treatment, and you are still being recorded.'

He pouted and shrugged his shoulders in an almost Gallic manner.

'The nurse will bind your hand,' I told him.

'Oh God,' he complained, gracelessly yet with a touch of humour.

I left the cubicle and met Stella out in the passage.

She said to me: 'That was tough stuff.' She meant it had been tough of me to do the operation in the antediluvian way.

'I hope it teaches him not to make a nuisance of himself.'

She handed me one of the forms to sign. I glanced at it and saw the name, Bruce Roecliffe.

Setting aside my reaction to that name, the story continues. I watched from a distance as Bruce Roecliffe emerged from the cubicle with his hand strapped. He was good-looking with his thick blond unruly hair. He walked like an athlete, lithely. He signalled to the woman, his companion, not Mary, and she stood up. Her hair was brown and long and hid her face, and she followed him towards the exit. They did not seem to be on very friendly terms.

He and that woman were not just friends. He was too masterful, she was too furtive. How were his fingers dislocated, in a row? Had that woman dislocated them? The news was not good for Mary – better for me.

Some days have passed since I wrote the above, and I have still not sorted out the pros and cons of my entry into one of the most disagreeable of relationships. Bruce Roecliffe wields power over Mary and, vicariously, over me. I am at his mercy as I have never been so at the mercy of any other man. I disliked him for good reasons before I knew who he was, I may also have disliked him at the urging of a sixth sense, and I took much more against him when I realised that Mary had at least to live with an errant husband, a spoilt brat, on whom my happiness depended. I shuddered to compare her wide apart, wide open, wide sweet eyes with those furious ice-blue eyes of his. I thought of him handing her a fat cheque, and her kissing him by way of thanks, and him demanding a more convincing proof of her gratitude. I thought of her humiliation, of her having to make do with the left-overs of other women, of the bribery and corruption involved. I pictured him padding along the passages of Wisteria Lodge, bent on teasing and torture. But I had done my bit of 'torture'. I had made him wince and squeal. I should not have broken with various codes of medical practice and relocated his fingers as painfully as possible. The irregularities multiply. Adultery is not a fairy story, nor a bedtime one as yet; but my aspirations in respect of Mary might turn out to be not the wildest of dreams. I have found myself not on the path of virtue, and waste my time on wondering if the end will ever justify the means.

My thought for this day is that work is good, leisure bad. We go to pieces if we have too little to do. I speak for myself – or write it, to be precise. I would not like to add to the difficulties of ill or disabled people, or the involuntary unemployed.

My MND patient died. Motor neurone disease is terrible, but in my experience is reserved by fate for the most heroic people.

May Day, the first day of the month of May, traditionally the time of village maidens dancing round maypoles in England, now the communist-socialist holiday that celebrates the murder of countless millions of class enemies.

Bank Holiday, no surgery, not much to do except count my mistakes; but the sun shone, so I drove out of Maeswell and walked in the Forest of Ashes. I seemed to be alone there, which was nice if not what I foolishly hoped for. I walked along a path or ride dappled by sunshine. Flowers showed off their colours and the young leaves on the trees boasted every shade of green. Birds sang, twittered, cawed, cooed, scolded and squawked. The rites of spring and regeneration were forging ahead. I sat down on a bank of mosses and buttercups, and these words formed in my head: 'I want gets nothing'.

However, curiosity refused to be renounced. I pinned down Audrey Fletcher in the rest-room and gave her a potted account of my brush with Bruce. Could she shed any light on it?

'Naughty Bruce,' she commented, frowning.

Then she asked me: 'What did she look like, the woman he was with on a Saturday night in the A and E?'

My answer was brown hair, a great deal of hair, and Audrey exclaimed: 'Oh dear!'

'Do you know her?'

'Not for certain, but she could be somebody as naughty as he is.'

'I see,' I said.

'No – you don't – any more than I do – and

I'm not going to cast the first stone, and you mustn't jump to conclusions – please!'

Audrey had spoken sharply.

I said okay, okay, and that I was sorry, because I liked Mary, and sorry I had lost my rag with her husband.

'He deserves it,' Audrey said, bustling out of range of further discussion.

The NHS, ruled by an unscientific temporary political boss and a vast bureaucracy, resembles China in the days of the Dowager Empress.

She rang me. She is returning the Tolstoy book tomorrow afternoon. My life is all believe-it-or-not.

Mary Roecliffe arrived at The Poor Cottage at four o'clock yesterday. She was shy with me, we were both shy. It was my fault, I showed too much emotion, greeted her too effusively, and had prepared tea with cucumber sandwiches.

I'm sorry to bother you,' she began, and when she saw the sandwiches she said, 'You shouldn't have – it's very kind of you – but I didn't mean ...'

'How are you?' I asked.

Oh, that cliché, that platitude, the question which elicits answers that people in general seldom listen to, that question fraught with deep meaning for lovers, who pose it with fear and trembling!

'I'm well, thank you,' she replied. 'How are you?'

'Fine,' I said, wishing it could have been, 'All the better for seeing you.'

She looked lovely, a lovely lady, a lady who was lovelier because of her blush; and agreeable, ready to respond to me, at once composed and eager, and not without humour, good humour.

She had read the book. She had not been able to stop reading it, and was grateful. We discussed it – she refreshed my memory – I had forgotten details. She was set on reading *War and Peace* and would buy it in London if it was unavailable in Maeswell. I said I hoped she would come to tea with me again even if she had no book to return, and we both laughed. Then I made the tea and we ate sandwiches to cover our confusion. She seemed to enjoy the two small sandwiches she ate while we spoke of her children and I revealed that I was a bachelor without any.

She said, breaking through some little barrier and forcing herself to say: 'You know you've written in the beginning of *Childhood, Boyhood and Youth*, there's something written in the front end-paper, and I thought it must be in your writing.'

'Because it's illegible?'

She saw the point, that doctors are supposed to have handwriting no one can decipher. I was anxious for a moment – could it be something scribbled by Iris? – and reached out for the book in order to look and see. It was the following quote from Tolstoy: 'The hero of my tale – whom I love with all the power of my soul, whom I have tried to portray in all his beauty, who has been, is, and will be beautiful – is Truth.' I remembered where Tolstoy had written it, and when I had, for that matter.

'Oh yes,' I said, and looked up from the book.

Her eyes were glistening.

'I'm sorry,' I said.

I was apologising for whatever it was that had made her sad.

'No, no, it's nothing – forgive me – that sentence is so moving. Truth is such a wonderful rare thing, isn't it?'

I agreed, and she continued.

'If you're a truthful person, you think when you're young that other people tell the truth, but they don't, often they don't, and it's a shock. You don't know where you are. Do you? Do you know people who don't tell the truth?'

'Oh yes. My patients lie like mad. I can never find out if they've taken the pills I've prescribed or how much they drink in an average day.'

She laughed and brushed away a tear with the back of a pretty index finger.

'I'm afraid I bore my children by begging them to speak the truth and nothing but. And I shouldn't, really, because they have enough to put up with.'

We talked for a few minutes, but I was not concentrating, had other things on my mind, and have forgotten what we talked about. Had she been referring to her marriage? Who had shocked her? Unexpectedly she announced that she should be going.

I over-reacted. I felt responsible, and a failure,

127

and probably showed my feelings as well as asking if she had to be in a hurry.

'My daughter – Melanie, who you know – will be finishing her dancing lesson, and I must be punctual or she'll worry.' Then she added: 'It's so peaceful in your home, and cosy with your books.'

'Will you come back one day?'

'Yes ... Yes,' she repeated, as though she could have said more.

She stood up and we moved in the direction of the door.

'Is Melanie well now?'

'Thank goodness, yes, she seems to be. That doctor in London, he had nothing new to say about her asthma, and she didn't take to him.'

We were veering in the direction of her husband, who had insisted on withdrawing Melanie from my care, and I inquired: 'Have Mr Roecliffe's fingers given any more trouble?'

She was either forgetful or puzzled.

'His dislocated fingers,' I jogged her memory.

'I don't understand,' she said.

But I did understand that I had dropped a brick and been indiscreet.

'It's nothing important, I did a running repair at the A and E the other day,' I said.

'What sort of repair? And what is A and E?'

'The Accident and Emergency Department at St Anne's Hospital. I work there on some weekend evenings. We all take turns to work there.'

'But what had happened to my husband?'

'I don't know – he'd dislocated two fingers –

it's easily done – and I put them back where they were meant to be. I only saw him for a minute or two, and we had no personal chit-chat.'

'Was he alone?'

'I don't know.'

'Did you say it was a weekend?'

'Yes.'

'Which day?'

'Saturday.'

'And when was it?'

I supplied the date.

'Oh,' she said or she sighed, and looking straight at me with a pained expression, she put an ironical gloss on the mischief I had inadvertently made: 'You're sure he wasn't attending a meeting in Paris?'

We managed to laugh.

She held out her hand for me to shake, but I clasped it in both of mine and said: 'Please come back soon, I'd love to see you again.'

She murmured, 'Thank you,' turned away, and I opened my front door and she walked into the street.

I cannot stop thinking about my brick and every thought enlarges it. Not content with clashing with the husband of darling Mary, I have drawn attention to the fact that she has been betrayed.

On second, third or fourth thoughts, it must have happened before. I mean, Mary would not have dismissed Bruce's infidelity with half a joke if she had not been aware of or even used to it. Owing to her disappointment and disillusion, she did not react to my news with incredulity, horror or hysteria. Self-interest is not moral: I was pleased to believe her marriage was unhappy. On the other hand, honesty reminded me that tears had flooded into her eyes because 'people', a 'person' maybe, her husband more than likely, told lies.

I gave Mary a couple of examples of the lies I am told by my patients. I could give her hundreds. Our Welfare State leads us into temptation, and money for jam does not deliver us from the evil of lying. Patient after patient has tried to convince me that they should receive handouts from the government because they are 'invalids' or 'incapable' of work. They want me to fib in writing that they are 'sick', should be allowed to park their cars where they please, deserve to be sent to a convalescent home, need cosmetic surgery, and so on. As a race, were we always so dishonest? Am I just getting older than I believe I am? Tolstoy was not wrong to love the truth – think of what befell his poor country, the Union of Socialist Soviet Republics, which ruled by lies.

Politics and sex go together, politics and love do not.

Here is a sad story or a cautionary tale. Bessie in Reception rang through to me during evening surgery to say a man wanting an emergency appointment seemed to be a phoney. He had said his name was John Smith and his home was in Yorkshire, but spoke with a West Country accent. Did he look mad or violent? Bessie answered no, so I told her to send him along. He was a mild-mannered man in his thirties, wearing a clean open-necked shirt and jeans. He asked for Viagra. He was very sorry to say it would help to keep his marriage on the rails. Yes, he was a married man. And he was the father of a son, a toddler. But he was squeamish, and he had yielded to the pleas of his wife, who was a nervous woman, to stay with and support her while their baby was born. It was traumatic. He was not meant to see everything, but he saw too much, and heard too much, his wife cursing and screaming her head off, and the doctor's and nurses' earthy exchanges. The consequence for him was that he left romance behind in the Labour Room at the hospital, and, worse, sexual desire. He was proud of his son, he was devoted to his wife, but he was unable to rise to the occasion of her marital overtures. I wrote the prescription. What would Mary think of Bruce Roecliffe and John Smith being almost bracketed together in my notebook?

I took tea with my mother at Silver Court before my surgery this evening. Walking there, I noticed a woman in the car park and, as doctors will, thought she must be or have been a patient of mine. I partly recognised her and cudgelled my memory. She was young-middle-age with a good figure, and was approaching her car. I suppose I stared at her, and she seemed to catch my eye, bent down to unlock the door of her car, and got into the driver's seat with her back turned to me. I remembered. She had a lot of straight brown hair, shoulder length, like a hedge – a hedge to hide behind. She was the woman in the A and E with Bruce Roecliffe – with or without Bruce, to be precise and imprecise simultaneously. She had hidden her face from me both in the waiting area and again in the car park at Silver Court. Did Ma know a woman who fitted her description?

'Oh yes,' Ma said. 'She's Vera Martin's daughter Pansy. She's often here. She's got that sort of hair, and at her age she should have it cut shorter and thinned.'

'Does she live nearby, is she married?' I asked.

Ma had beans to spill. Pansy was accident-prone. She married a man called Egbert Doughty, an unsuccessful engineer and really, as Ma put it, 'ditchwater'. She produced two children, a delinquent boy, and a spiteful girl. The Doughty home was poor and miserable by all accounts. But Pansy made matters worse by picking a lover who was even worse than her husband. Apparently he is rich and spoilt, had taken her up and soon dropped her, and she had pursued him and come in for rough treatment – he was married, of course. There had been a bust-up not long ago, when she attacked him physically and he had beaten her black and blue. Vera Martin worried

132

rather publicly about her daughter – she feared divorce was in the offing, and Pansy would have no means of support. Her lover had promised her the earth, and that was exactly what she would be left with.

Ma asked me: 'Why are you interested in Pansy?'

'I'm not,' I replied. 'But I always wonder what women mean when they speak of being beaten up. Some patients of mine consult me if their hair's been pulled or their faces have been slapped.'

'It wasn't like that for Pansy. She had to have her breast scanned because he'd hit her there, and she had ribs broken by his kicking.'

I obtained this information under false pretences. In London I treated half a dozen women with serious injuries inflicted by their so-called lovers who were drunk, drugged, sadistic, moronic, or inadequate and feeble. I had not told Ma, had misled her, because I was keen to know more about Bruce Roecliffe and the sort of husband he might be to Mary. He had been nasty in the A & E; but he spoke the Queen's English, was not a pleb or a prole, and dressed expensively. That he could torture a woman and risk giving her breast cancer, and break her bones, was bad news. Mary was married to a violent bully. The extenuating factor might be that Pansy née Martin had infuriated him. When the beating occurred? My guess is that she and Bruce had a row and a wrestling match, she bent back his fingers and dislocated them, and after he had been treated at St Anne's Hospital with her in attendance they had driven somewhere, indoors or outdoors, and he had caused her GBH – Mary, meanwhile, labouring under the impression that he was in Paris.

More summer colds than life-saving crises. I suffer nonetheless from a double 'whammy'. First, George Mills, the antediluvian heart-throb of Silver Court, was taken ill and I attended: nothing much wrong, mostly the ailment known as *anno domini* – perhaps one of the romantic female residents had gained access to his bedroom. Anyway, he revived and shook a knarled finger at me. I was not a 'proper' doctor, he said, because I looked in my computer instead of practising the art of 'diagnosis by the eye', and I did not examine his tongue, tonsils, glands in the neck, sound his chest back and front, or test his reflexes, as was always *de rigueur*, part of the etiquette of medical practice, in the good old days. Secondly, Robert Chimes came down to stay the night at The Poor Cottage – I could put it another way, he came down on me like a ton of bricks. He scolded me for not surfing the internet, not doing emails, not having a modern mobile, not text-messaging, and not having the wherewithal to play videos, CDs or DVDs. Unwisely I had let him in on the secret of Mary Roecliffe, and he roasted me for loving a woman who should not love me, for my masochism and addiction to failure, for having stuck in the rut of Iris and for not letting the dead bury the dead, and for not realising that *les belles dames sans merci* were no longer on the menu and the twenty-first century is not the age of chivalry.

My reading has gone phut recently. It is again restricted to pill-makers' adverts and newspaper headlines. My literary leanings boil down to imagining Mary's reactions to *War and Peace*. And nothing has happened worthy of a note in this book – no maiden imprisoned in a Gothic castle has let down her golden tresses for me to fondle.

I wrote the sentence above too soon. Today, Saturday, this afternoon, there was a sale of work in our church hall and Bill Wetherby had asked me to put in an appearance. I walked through the churchyard in hot sunshine round about three. The hall, like the church, is Victorian, but has been given some sliding glass doors facing west, which were open wide. The trestle tables displaying goods for sale were inside the hall, some tea-tables with chairs were outside, on a grassy lawn away from the graves. I had a few words with Bill, then with his wife Ada, who presided over the arts and crafts exhibits, mostly daubs by children and wooden mice with leather ears and tails. There were other stalls for clothing, jam and cakes, fruit and vegetables. A good many people had turned up, and many of them were my patients. I was talking and shaking hands, and refusing offers of cups of tea, in the sunshine on the lawn, when I saw Mary. She was with her two children and two older people. She wore that seductive thin light-coloured summer apparel for women, and a broad-brimmed straw hat at an angle. We saw each other at the same time. Her face lit up – or I chose to think it did – as mine certainly had. We met in the crowd. She gave me her hand more to hold than to shake, and she smiled at me warmly enough to melt hearts colder than mine. She indicated Melanie and introduced me to Tom, and then introduced me to her parents. Tom is a wan child of seven or thereabouts, Melanie seemed scarcely to recognise me. Mary's parents are called Warden – she would have been Mary Warden. Her father is a tall handsome polite man, her mother has a friendly smile. Talking was not easy. She said that two of Tom's paintings were for sale – they had been viewing them – and I said something about *War and Peace*. Her parents mentioned the lucky weather. Then Bruce Roecliffe appeared. He was shouldering his way through and called harshly to Mary as if she had been a dog. He was still at a little distance. Mary ignored his summons – she commented on by ignoring it – and said: 'I've finished the book and wish I hadn't.' Tom interrupted. He was tugging at his mother's clothes and pleading with her: 'Dad's waiting for us, Dad's waiting.' Mary said to him, 'I know.' But Bruce had not waited. He stormed up and expostulated, 'For God's sake, Mary, come on!' She introduced me cleverly, that is non-committally, for she cannot have wanted him to know that she knew about his fingers and philandering. She said, 'This is Dr Selaby.' He flashed a glance at me, mumbled, 'Hi!', turned his back and strutted off, calling, 'You kids, get a move on!' Mary asked me, 'May I ring you?' I answered, 'Please!' Mrs Warden said as she passed me, 'We have our marching orders,' and Mr Warden raised his eyebrows, signifying a mixture of disapproval and resignation. I re-entered the hall, crossing to Ada Wetherby's trestle table, and bought the pictures by Tom Roecliffe.

It was an unsettling encounter. Bruce Roecliffe is or has an unquiet spirit – how did he marry a woman with quiet eyes? I know the type – doctors have to try to diagnose souls as well as the diseases of bodies – and I see signs of the warlock stirring in Bruce. He sets my teeth on edge. Such people merit scientific investigation: what is it that forces them to create bad feeling, jagged edges, exasperation, antipathy?

For the record, I have shuffled awkward patients out of my consulting room and into a colleague's, and the colleague in question has noticed nothing untoward or disagreeable. Yet there seems to be an antonym or counterpoint to love at first sight. Personally, I would avoid Bruce like the plague if I could, if it were not for our inter-dependency.

Tom's paintings were upsetting, too. One was of a house on fire, the other of a tree falling down.

The subjects were fearful and the colours used were lurid. Tom had not looked like a country boy in the church garden – no touch of sun, no freckles. Melanie was pale and shrinking. I suspected they were frightened by their father; but I was frightened of mine at their age – and the vogue of calling fathers by their Christian names and not being frightened of them has cost modern mothers dear. The psyches of children defeat analysis more thoroughly – if possible – than adult psyches do. A distressing comparison struck me: Melanie and Tom were reminiscent of the children in Henry James' ghost story, *The Turn of the Screw*.

No telephone call from Mary in these last days.

Another resolve not to break up a marriage. Another attempt to justify my hypocrisy. Another prayer to be forgiven. Again, and almost, I dare to reproach God for enabling us to love even in vain, also for giving some of us a monogamous instinct; but I blame myself for Iris, for Rose, and potentially for Mary. The Hippocratic Oath, which I swore, is all for morality, and I have stumbled into the amoral modern jungle. Actually, the Age of Chivalry produced a code of love – I remember reading a list of its rules – including one that would answer Robert and comfort me if my memory could be relied on. The love that is dedicated wholeheartedly and without self-interest to the service of the beloved, the rule goes, transcends other undertakings and bonds.

Life is cheap nowadays, yet nowadays modern states levy crippling taxes to pay for the welfare of the people and the prolongation of life. The dearth of logic compounds confusion. Bombs turn out to be easy to make, nitwits queue up to be suicide bombers, and governments drop bigger better ones while legislating against the death penalty for heinous murder. It seems that governments only kill innocent people. No wonder morality is a muddle and the end is probably nigh! If time is short, I would like to state here and now and without a doubt that I loved Iris in haste and regret those eleven years at leisure, and will regret their outcome for ever. I mean my love of Mary at least to be different. The idea of love without self-interest would worry any red-blooded man of my age; but the empathy and sympathy between me and Mary promise that our interest in each other could be fully satisfied when our circumstances and scruples permit.

Trouble at mill: Denis Woods may be sued. Conscientious Denis may be sued for negligence. The story beggars belief. Denis had a troublesome middle-aged patient who had a troublesome daughter of twenty-three: mother a well-to-do divorcee called Anne Collett, daughter called Micky, short for Michaela, and father of Micky an expat. Micky drifted in and out of relationships, jobs, dwellings, psychiatrists' clutches, rehab clinics and financial scrapes. One night she went out with a new boyfriend, got drunk or drugged or both, agreed to go back to his flat, undressed, got into bed with him, changed her mind, said no, and he had his way with her. She returned home, to her mother's house, said she had been raped, and her mother summoned Denis, who turned out in the middle of the night and drove ten miles to where the Colletts live.

Micky told her tale reluctantly, she was honest enough not to blame the boy exclusively, and only concerned in case she would have a baby. Denis gave medical help and his opinion, which was that rape had not occurred, since Micky had gone too far to have the right to draw back, and she had not left the boyfriend's bed after saying no for two subsequent hours. Mrs Collett raged at him, but he could and would not change his mind, and he departed. Mrs Collett then summoned the police; the next day the police contacted Denis and agreed with his reading of the evidence; and the case seemed to be closed. However, a feminist organisation took a different view. It paid a solicitor to write Denis a threatening letter stating that he was negligent to have influenced the police in the matter of the rape victim Michaela Collett, who was denied a thorough investigation of the crime. Denis wrote back that the lady in question failed a breath test several hours after the alleged rape. He had also taken a blood sample, so far untested, which, he was sure, would show traces of illegal substances. Both tests were authorised by Miss Collett's signature. He added that if legal proceedings should be instigated, he would cross-petition that the feminists were challenging his professional integrity on behalf of a contrary over-age nymphet and tease, guilty on several counts. Denis still fears the feminists – they have money to burn, he says, and the militants have no better understanding of right and wrong than male chauvinists.

The Cunninghams again invited me to dine, I accepted the invitation, and now I already feel their food sticking in my throat. Penny issued the invitation. Since then Frank has told me the names of the other guests. My opposite number is as yet unknown. People called Perry are coming, Victor is a dermatologist with a practice in London as well as in Tinbury, and Shell is a pretty young woman with an interest in the arts. The other couple, who will make eight of us in all, are Bruce and Mary Roecliffe.

Bruce will be the guest of honour. He has apparently given money to St Christopher's Hospice, where Frank is one of the visiting team of doctors. Frank thinks Bruce is a philanthropist and good fellow.

This dinner party preys on my mind. Romance relies on privacy. Romantic love is the opposite of 'social' love that has to show itself off. Society, high and low, is a waste of time and energy for a person in love – and almost the same applies for a teetotaller. Society is a marriage market or a dating agency for ungregarious souls, or it is nothing but a bore. It also serves as a business forum, where useful contacts can be made and insider deals done. I write as an overworked doctor, a man in love, and a temperamental recluse – three good reasons not to go to dinner with the Cunninghams and have to endure the company of my beloved together with her legal lord and master.

Life seems to have been simplified by a generation younger than mine. I refer to four of my patients in their twenties, all occasional churchgoers, who have supplied me with autobiographical information. Molly Prentice justified her desertion of her hard-working husband, who was devoted to their children, by saying she had always wanted to be a single mother – she was awarded custody of the children. Jane West justified her divorce proceedings by explaining that she was fed up with having to ask her husband for money, she was hoping the courts would grant her a fat capital sum and index-linked alimony. John Walker walked out of his marriage because he was tired of his brood. Adrian Lucas left his wife at the airport where they were catching a flight to their honeymoon destination. The common excuse for bad marital behaviour is 'I no longer love him or her' – which is a contradiction and retraction of everything they have said and done in the period of courtship, and of all they have solemnly sworn in church.

* * *

We congregated on Saturday evening at the Cunninghams' in Larkspur. We had been asked for eight. The evening was grey and rainy, English summer weather. I was the first to arrive, and was greeted by both Frank and Penny – she powdered and painted and wearing a dress that revealed too much crinkled flesh. She hugged me, Frank was gravely welcoming, and they told me that Mrs Minksoft would be my neighbour at dinner – I would be between Mrs Minksoft and Shell Perry, the dermatologist's mate, whom Penny said I would adore. The Perrys were the next arrivals, he a bald benevolent tough-talking sixty-year-old, she a fortyish redhead with wet-looking lips. Mrs Minksoft was late, and blamed her chauffeur. She is small and dark, rotund, and looks as rich as she is supposed to be. The Roecliffes were late – Mary apologised, he did not.

When Frank introduced me to the Perrys, he – Victor Perry – passed a remark I had heard annually since my childhood: he said, 'Not very promising weather for Wimbledon.' Shell Perry had a racier line in small talk. She said: 'Are you a gynaecologist? ... What a pity, I have a laugh with gynaes ... Not married? ... And no partner?' Mrs Minksoft is a Hungarian chatterbox. She said: 'A doctor, my dear! My husband is a doctor, too. He has a doctorate from Oxford – in literature, my dear – but he writes nothing except cheques, he is a doctor of money, which is good luck for many people, but especially for me.' She laughed at her own joke loudly and showing

143

the gold crowns of her mouthful of teeth. Frank introduced me to the Roecliffes. Mary and I shook hands for longer than was necessary and two words were exchanged along with smiles: she said to me, 'Hullo,' and I said 'Hullo' to her. She then reminded Bruce that he had met me at the fête in the grounds of my church. He said, 'How are you?', and waved a hand at me dismissively but not exactly rudely.

I cannot describe women's clothes; suffice it to say that Mary was well-dressed for dinner in a town in the country in summer, and that her appearance qualified for those sweet unfashionable compliments, fresh, clean, dignified, ethereal. Bruce wore white trousers, a blazer, an open-necked shirt and a scarf or handkerchief loosely knotted round his neck. He had dash, I give him that, he was also flash; and, although men are supposed never to know whether or not other men are attractive to women, I could see that with his thick tangle of golden hair, aquiline features, bold blue eyes and carnivorous smile, he exuded sex appeal.

Bruce and Mrs Minksoft were acquainted. He addressed her as 'Minx' and she called him 'wicked'. Bruce and Shell Perry were more than acquaintances. He was her 'sweety-pie' and she was his 'Poppet', and they kissed cheek-to-cheek, laughing as if at a charade. We drank our dry martinis – Mary, talking to the dermatologist, refused hers – and Penny bustled in and led the ladies into the dining-room. Shell Perry walked ahead of me. In view of later events, I must record that her flimsily clad back view was pleasing and that she wore no discernible knickers.

The Cunninghams' dining room is oblong, and we sat as follows under the Montague Dawson prints of great yachts racing in wide seas: Frank at the end of the table near the window, Mary on his right, Victor Perry next to Mary, Penny Cunningham next to Victor and near the kitchen door, Bruce Roecliffe on Penny's right, Shell between Bruce and me, and Mrs Minksoft on my right and Frank's left. The important thing so far as I was concerned was that I could look across the table at Mary – I was not sorry not to be sitting next to her, I would have been shy and we would have had to make polite conversation.

Whatever the laws of social etiquette appertaining to dinner parties, the Cunninghams broke them, probably unconsciously. Each chose to talk to his and her more attractive neighbour, Frank to Mary rather than to Mrs Minksoft and Penny to Bruce rather than to Victor Perry. As a result, for quite a time, Mrs Minksoft on one side of the table and Victor the dermatologist on the other were left out conversationally and sat in silence, eating the bridge-rolls on their side-plates. More difficulties were caused by Frank rising to his feet to pour out white and red wines, and by Penny leaping to hers in order to give orders in the kitchen.

However, alcohol and food generated good

will. We had avocados with vinaigrette to start with, sole in a white sauce with grapes as main course, prune mould and vanilla ice-cream for pudding, and cheese straws. Shell Perry told me that Australian men were even worse lovers than Englishmen, she said the corks dangling from the brims of Australian male headgear distracted women from the matter in hand. Mrs Minksoft aired her opinion that her husband Rudolph must have given more money to Frank for his Hospice than Bruce Roecliffe could have done, and therefore she should have been sitting on Frank's right instead of Mary. Victor Perry roared with laughter at a joke he had cracked with Penny Cunningham, Mrs Minksoft shouted down the table at Bruce, Frank was passing round a decanter of port, and Mary and I exchanged a conspiratorial glance or two.

We were still there, but sitting less formally. Shell Perry had half-turned to Bruce Roecliffe and he – on her left – had also half-turned and had his right arm resting on the back of her chair. They were laughing – others were laughing, but Shell and Bruce were laughing in a nearly lascivious way. All of a sudden I guessed, realised, that as his left arm was under the table and her legs were extended in its direction, he was caressing her where a more respectable woman would have worn knickers. My reaction was to look at Mary. I saw, at once, that she had seen. Her countenance had somehow solidified, was stony, like a sculpture. Then her eyes met mine, beaming at me a message of pain and misery. A moment later, deliberately but as if by accident, she pushed back her chair. Penny had the tact to stand up and shepherd all the ladies, including not much of a lady, out of the dining-room.

Frank is old-fashioned, he believes in giving his guests for dinner the chance to 'wash their hands', and each sex to have a chinwag without interruption by the other. We four men were alone in the dining-room, Frank, self, Bruce and Victor Perry, and the decanter of port was rotating clockwise. Frank thanked Bruce again for his donation to St Christopher's Hospice. Bruce's answer was an unexpected diatribe, and to the best of my memory went like this: 'Thanks for feeding us, Frank, but – sorry! – I'm here to complain. Having two other captive quacks is all to the good. 1 want to blast off at the National Health Service. You lot let the bloody politicians create the bloody monster – hadn't any of you ever heard of Dr Frankenstein? Over fifty-odd years the monster's grown way beyond control. Politicians are windbags, they're not competent to run anything, countries or a health service, they're the puppets of bureaucrats, and bureaucrats are like rabbits, only good at reproducing themselves. You'll tell me the monster's beautifully dressed, but I'm telling you it's stark naked. To hell with pious hopes and downright lies: politics can't beat nature. No legislation can stop people being ill. No society should presume it can keep everyone healthy and alive, and no society can afford that sort of nonsense. Our hospitals are

147

fever-pits – if you go into hospital relatively well you come out ill or dead. They're filthy. And who are the cleaners and the kitchen staff, are they taught hygiene, are they disciplined by being hired and fired freely by a matron or a leading doctor? Tell me another! And in the A & E, drug addicts and drunks shouldn't be treated as if they were decent people, they should be thrown in a cell until they're sober and a doctor or a nurse has the time and inclination to deal with them. Better late than never, why not withdraw your labour and force the politicians to think again? Wake up! Make people pay if they can for your services – pay if they can, pay at least a deposit, pay up for missing appointments, pay in full for misbehaving! Stop conniving with the criminals milking the benefits system! Cut the hypocrisy – people never will be equal – let the rich and the poor be what they are and wish to be! No sharp intakes of breath, please – I'm not being original or saying anything extraordinary! It's common knowledge – free health services ruin a country – the idea of free health is tempting fate – and the Welfare State's a slippery slope. You doctors should damn well pull yourselves together and start cleaning out the bloody stables!'

We rejoined the ladies briefly. Because I could not help Mary, I only longed to be away and at home. The sight of her suffering towards the end of dinner, and the thought of her living with a man so randy and shameless, so dogmatic and oppressive as Bruce Roecliffe, got me down.

148

How could he, how could she? That he talked some sense about the Health Service did not compensate for his abrasive delivery. The dermatologist, Victor Perry, had two good reasons to remove Shell from the scene of the party: he was unamused by Bruce and had called him a vandal and a hooligan, terms perhaps also applicable to Bruce's friendship with his wife. Bruce himself took his leave brusquely, he seemed to have shot his bolts in the dining room; Mary followed him out, and I followed Mary.

Frank and Penny stood in the lit doorway, bidding us good night in crestfallen tones. The dinner had gone wrong, and they sensed it. I waved goodbye to the Perrys, and Bruce nodded at me, and Mary addressed me in an undertone when I opened the passenger door of the Roecliffes' car.

'Can I see you?'

'Any time.'

'Tomorrow at four?'

'Yes!'

She got into the car, and Bruce drove off fast, scattering the Cunninghams' gravel.

Today is the next day. It is evening now. At four o'clock I saw Mary passing my sitting-room window, and opened my front door. I closed the door quickly, and we faced each other in the dark little room. We smiled, were relieved, were almost happy, were together and safe.

She had not seemed to be hurried, but there was urgency in our exchanges.

149

I thanked her for being with me.

'No – thank you – but I shouldn't be here –
I'll have to leave you soon.'

Would she not have tea?

'No – don't worry.'

'It's Sunday, not a day for dancing classes.'

'They're having tea with friends, my children,
and I must go and join the party. I must be sure
to pick them up and take them home before...'

'Before what?'

'Can you tell me something? What did Bruce
do when the men were alone last night?'

'He made a speech.'

'What about?'

'About the NHS and its failings. He wanted
us to put it right.'

'Was he rude?'

'Not quite – rough – and excitable.'

'I don't want him to collect the children from
their party. He scares them.'

'Won't you sit down and rest?'

'No – I can't – it would have been nice, if
I'd come here to discuss *War and Peace*. I just
wanted to see you again and be in your soothing
atmosphere.'

'It's the same for me.'

'No – no – what I've told you isn't the whole
truth. You ought to know it's a mistake to be
friends with a woman who's having matrimonial
problems.'

'I can't help being your friend.'

'No – thank you – but you mustn't, we mustn't
– you're on quicksand – and I want to rescue

you while there's still a chance – I came to say goodbye.'

'Please don't say it.'

'Yes – we're a might-have-been, you must see that.'

'But I ask very little, I expect nothing much.'

'It couldn't be, it wouldn't work.'

'Please, Mary.'

'We're strangers – in one way we are – you have no idea of the trouble you could be getting into – honestly, I'm thinking of you – only of you.'

'I know – I do know that – and it's why I can't help loving you.'

'Oh God!'

She uttered the words in the form of a small scream, and headed for the door. I touched her arm, a touch not a restraint, our first physical contact since her arrival, and she stopped, almost froze.

'Can I write to you? Can I ever speak to you?'

'No – no, definitely.'

'Mary!'

'Give me time,' she said.

'How much time?'

'A month.'

'Will you communicate after a month?'

'I promise.'

'She reached for the door handle, but I stepped forward to open it. We did not speak again. I watched her walking away until she turned the corner where the churchyard ends.

PART THREE

NOTEBOOK FIVE

When Mrs Peele told me that she was engaged to her future husband Ron for nine years, I took it personally. A long time to wait, I remarked. She explained that they had been saving in order to buy a home of their own.

Mrs Peele cleans my Poor Cottage on Mondays and Fridays, removes my dirty washing and brings it back clean, changes my sheets, copes with refuse, and buys household necessities. I seldom see her, but by her works I know her. She does not bother, nag, ruin or bore me. Why should I want a wife?

We both happened to be at The Poor Cottage the other morning, Mrs Peele and self, and, following on from her revelation about the length of her engagement, I ventured to ask if Ron was worth waiting for. She said: 'Well, we've been lucky because of knowing we were comfortable together.'

Mary is obviously not comfortable with Bruce. I am and believe I would be comfortable with Mary. The moot point is whether or not she would be comfortable with me in the longer term. On Sunday afternoon she was very distressed, and I passed one of the acid tests of courtship,

I was not completely undone, nonplussed, infected with or defeated by her distress.

But I am sad, although a few days are not nine years. And I worry for her with more reason than she has to worry unselfishly for me.

The pains of romantic love are not much fun for mature persons. Shakespeare was not wrong to make Romeo and Juliet children.

To pass the time, my free time which is not much but seems longer because Mary is not on my horizon, I again picked up *Dead Souls*. The gloomy title matched my mood, but it is misleading, a misnomer. The first 'book' of three is comedy, fun, joy and delight, an exception to every rule, a fantasy of genius, non-stop entertainment of the highest order. Gogol, the author, refers to it as a 'poem' – and so it is. The other two 'books' are as peculiar as the first in that they are dull, stupid and unreadable – Gogol is thought not to have written them although they appear under his name. He was born in 1809 and died in 1852, aged forty-one. He published his first writings at his own expense. He was extremely prolific in his short life, and became one of the great writers. He was not a 'normal' man, and never happy. I wonder if Mary would like his book.

A doctor's work is never done. However sad or unwell he or she may be, he or she is almost bound to have to treat a patient who is sadder and iller than he or she is. The real doctor's dilemma is how to be always more sorry for patients than for himself or herself.

The telephone is a blessing for old people, but a curse for those who are older than old, and for their relations, friends, tradesmen and doctors. Ma was telling me that Joyce, the daytime 'warden' at Silver Court, was driven almost to drink by nonagenarian Laura Henbey, who has developed an aversion to returning the receiver to its cradle: result, Joyce is rung in her office repeatedly by Laura's cronies wanting to know if she is alive and, if so, why is her telephone dead or emitting the engaged signal. They have fixed her up with an antique instrument of the kind used by Laura in the 1920s – it stands twelve inches high; but I understand the improvement is not great.

A pile-up on the main road, a 4 × 4 driven by a youth crashed through the barrier between two carriageways and ploughed into a small car containing four members of a single family, OAP car owner, his wife, sister and sister-in-law. I was called out to help to revive the youth, but he was already in an ambulance when I arrived. He was not badly hurt, the four other casualties were dead. A female journalist buttonholed me and spoke of the 'tragedy'. I returned, 'Why do you journalists insist on getting everything wrong? This isn't a tragedy, it's a crime scene.' The youth is a local criminal aged nineteen. He stole the

4 × 4 from a yard of secondhand cars for sale. The vehicle was not roadworthy and had no Road Tax and was uninsured. The youth, who had no licence and drove it too fast, was drunk and drugged by cannabis. The other car was in the slow lane when it was hit. Its driver was a retired Minister of the Methodist Church. His descendants and those of his sister and sister-in-law will receive no money from any insurance company. The youth will be sentenced to a rest cure in prison. In my opinion he should pay the ultimate penalty for his offence and the harm he has done. If or when the politicians reinstate capital punishment by one method or another, I will gladly pull the hangman's handle or administer the lethal injection.

Love is blind, but should I be straining my eyes to see the trap that Mary warned me not to fall into? She referred to her marriage: I have assumed all along that it is problematical – she would not have reciprocated my overtures to any extent if she had been exclusively occupied by wifehood. That Bruce is a serial adulterer would not surprise me – I witnessed his pass at Shell Perry under the Cunninghams' dining table at which his wife was sitting. He can be grouped with the cohorts of horrible husbands, and might be a horrible father too – she said he frightened his children. He is certainly a bully – he tried to bully three doctors, one of which was his host and old enough to be his father. In short, Bruce Roecliffe is not perfect, but had Mary meant that he was insanely jealous and might try to murder me?

*　*　*

From my glass house I ought not to throw stones at Bruce for being an adulterer, and I have no proofs of the extent of his promiscuity. However, loving another man's wife is a novelty for me, and I cannot resist the urge to analyse it. The main difference between a love affair and adultery is the legal aspect – legal in innumerable senses, according to the laws of God, of the land, of tradition, etiquette and human nature, because the adulterer is trying to steal somebody from somebody else, alienate someone's affections, hurt someone's feelings, appropriate a possession of more or less value, take advantage, cheat and win the game. Are there extenuating factors? Surely the unhappiness of a wife would excuse a readiness to be rescued and released from durance, duress, and violence of one sort or another. Mary's morals are irreproachable, I believe, but is she a wife battered and brainwashed by Bruce who has a screw loose? How I yearn to be able to speak to her, hear her voice on the telephone, ask if she is all right, or pour out my feelings on paper, in a letter, in letters!

My dreams of love that is pure if adulterous are rudely interrupted by battles of the war of the sexes waged in my consulting room. Women's ailments I pass on to Audrey Fletcher or to a specialist if I can, but often I am too late to stifle a tale of woe or terror. Women are apt to book an appointment for one reason, pain in a toe or a congested cough, when they really want to see me for another. They are bewildered by their partners' sexual requirements. A woman asked me if it was right and proper of her husband to wash her from head to foot with Dettol before and after intercourse. Women have asked me if the following were acceptable and should be accepted: a white honeymoon, a partner with satyriasis, perverse practices, sex exclusively on the kitchen table, oral sex that goes too far, his arousal by her pain, physical assault? Several women have described marriages and even partnerships that were never loving, sex that was rare and disagreeable, pregnancies that were simply awful, and motherhood that was drudgery. For all classes of persons, upper, middle or lower, to be the weaker sex is dangerous. Admittedly men have consulted me about women who, with cruel words, sarcasm, mockery and contrariness, have virtually castrated them. But I dredge up these dirty memories because of Mary and my suspicions of Bruce.

Today Frank Cunningham and I found ourselves together in the rest-room. I had written to thank Penny for dinner, and I now thanked Frank. His gesture conveyed the message that thanks were out of order. He was dissatisfied by his evening of entertainment and expressed his dissatisfaction characteristically.

He asked me if I had been acquainted with Mr Perry. When I said no, he said that he had never before met Mr Perry's wife, Shell, who seemed to be a lively lady. I indicated agreement.

160

'Yes, well,' Frank continued, 'Penny tells me she was not behaving in a modest manner. Were you aware of anything of that sort?'

I did not mince my words in reply, I was unwilling to protect Bruce.

'Good gracious,' Frank exclaimed.

He continued: 'Bruce Roecliffe blotted his copybook twice over in that case.'

We discussed his – Bruce's – post-prandial opinion of and advice to the medical profession. Frank was against all of it, and squashed my tentative support of one or two of his ideas.

'However,' Frank changed the subject. 'However, I have a third concern in respect of Bruce Roecliffe. He has given money to St Christopher Hospice, he did so before he came to live down here, and he has since then. He's been generous, I grant, but recently I've heard of a case of possible malpractice. He wangled money out of an old friend of ours, who lives in Silver Court and is acquainted with your mother, invested it in some speculative scheme, and, when it was lost, informed her in an off-hand and casual manner.'

'But isn't he a stockbroker? I thought he was, and that his business dealings were regulated by official bodies in the City of London.'

'No, he's a financial adviser, and seems to have the right to do as he pleases.'

'I suppose your friend was rash to hand over more money that she could afford.'

'Yes, but Bruce was wrong to have obtained her money by saying he could increase it, by investing in a speculative way, and wrong again to react to the loss as he did. Our friend needed income, she's too old to hope to benefit from slow capital growth. He acted at least irresponsibly, and has broken laws of natural justice. I wonder why he donates to our Hospice – how guilty is his conscience? The pressing question is whether or not we should continue to accept his donations.'

I had no answer for Frank, and many new questions for myself; but meanwhile I paid an urgent visit to Silver Court.

In reply to my cautious questions Ma told me that Lisbet Tinnislea as well as Gabriella Shelby were friendly with Bruce Roecliffe. Lisbet is another resident at Silver Court, pretty in an old-fashioned way, according to Ma, and Austrian by birth – I have not met her. Whether or not Lisbet has entrusted money to Bruce, she has not publicly complained of losing it; and Gabriella still seems to be pleased with him both financially and personally.

'He's an odd man,' I commented carefully.

'I was introduced to him the other day. He's good-looking, I can see why the ladies fall for him.'

I could have done without the last remark.

I asked: 'Was he after your money, Ma?'

'Well – he gave me his card.'

'Don't ask him to invest your money, don't on any account!'

'Is he a crook?'

'I don't know that, I don't know it for certain, but I'd prefer you to play safe.'

'He has a glittering eye.'

'You always say that's a bad sign.'

'It's not a good one.'

'What does it signify, Ma?'

She shrugged her shoulders, and asked: 'Are you friends?'

'Acquaintances.'

'Is he married?'

'Yes.'

'With children?'

'Yes, a girl and a boy.'

'Are you a friend of his wife?'

'You're too sharp, Ma!'

'Is she your special friend?'

'Maybe.'

'Now it's my turn to tell you to play safe. I wouldn't like you to be on the wrong side of him.'

'No ... I wouldn't like that either. He's so odd he could do anything, and I feel protective of Mary Roecliffe.'

'Clever women protect themselves.'

'Thanks for the advice, Ma.'

'What advice am I to give Lisbet and Gabriella?'

'If he's got their money they should try to get it back. They could say they need it for a young relative's wedding or an old relative's funeral. Don't mention my name, please!'

'I won't. And I mustn't alarm them. What has Bruce done that you don't approve of, apart from marrying Mary?'

'He made mistakes for the friend of a friend of mine. I'm not saying he stole the money. He probably bought shares that went down instead of up.'

'Is that serious?'

'Serious enough.'

'Anything else?'

'I think he's dangerous.'

Robert Chimes again stayed the night. When he had stopped making mockery of my dedication, I asked him if he had ever come across or heard of Bruce. He tapped his forehead with his fingers and supplied the following. There had been some financial jiggery-pokery that landed Roecliffe in a court of law, and then he was cited in an unsavoury divorce case – Roecliffe had seduced a wife, the husband divorced her, and she came to a sticky end, in a car crash or by suicide.

'When was that, the divorce case?'

'Oh, five or six years ago.'

In other words, Bruce had been unfaithful to Mary not long after they were married, judging by Melanie aged nine and Tom aged seven.

I have not lost my nerve or my patience. Something precious and priceless passed between me and Mary at once, when we first set eyes on each other, an emotion unique inasmuch as I had experienced nothing like it before and expect never to experience again – for lightning does not strike the same spot twice – and convinced me that she is my fate, come what may. I remember with a surge of gratitude the awareness that my search for the other better half of myself

164

was over, and my recognition of that commitment which is the sole agent of peace. But the 'buts' have raised their ugly heads. To mix my metaphors, the sharp points of common sense puncture and deflate. How long, oh Lord? I have nothing whatsoever to count on. Unhappy marriages have connections with creaking doors that never fall off their hinges. I have no knowledge of what I am up against, the history, the past, the characters, the future. I do not like to think of my relationship with Mary as a siege, yet I begin to consider a future of digging myself in and sitting out the time it will take for her to surrender. I must not pollute love with obstinacy – love is above trying to prove Ma and Robert wrong.

It is the middle of the third week of the month of our semi-voluntary 'separation'. I have not yielded to the temptation to break in on Mary largely because I do not know how to, and she has not relented – *War and Peace* remains undiscussed. This afternoon I went for another walk in the Forest of the Ashes. Nature was celebrating summer. I saw young rabbits with flirty white scuts, grey squirrels played hide-and-seek with me, a weasel sprinted by like a hyperactive toy, and magpies chuckled murderously. Adult creatures were being run ragged by the demands of their babies, and the trees were heavily pregnant with leaves and fruits. The scene could be called happy, if happiness is a feature of the wildlife experience with its non-stop struggle to survive; but I felt sad on account of a patient. Alec

Whitehead was a new patient – he limped into my consulting room yesterday, looking dreadful. He is a scholar, author of biographies, dignified, polite. He was so sorry to bother me. He told me he had AIDS, and how long he expected to live. His hometown was London, he had been treated there for several years, and had come to Maeswell to be nursed by his mother, who has a house in King Arthur's Terrace. He showed me his medication, and wondered if I could think of any medicine to make his last days either more bearable or fewer. He was precise, not emotional. He was not only new to me, he was my first AIDS case – in my London hospital those patients were directed to a specialised department. I offered him a few strong painkillers. He was grateful, and seemed to want to unburden himself. He said he had probably contracted the infection without knowing it when he was thirty-seven, thirteen years ago. It had cut short his career, also finished his love life, and forced him, who had lived openly with a man, to keep the secret that he was ill and potentially infectious. He had been his mother's blue-eyed boy, he said, he had been going to win fame for her sake, but she understood him, she understood everything.

At this stage I asked if he had ever been bisexual, and he answered, 'Never!'

'Thank goodness for that,' I said.

He reproached me gently.

'I would have liked to be bisexual, but I wasn't. We think bisexuality's natural. We think there's very little difference between homosexuality, bisexuality and heterosexuality. We use words like copulation and fornication to describe our acts of love and passion.'

I tried to express sympathy.

He said: 'I'm lucky to have lived for fifty wonderful years.'

I urged him to come back for another prescription of the painkillers if need be.

'Oh, I don't think I'll need more,' he replied with his wisp of a smile.

Acquired Immune Deficiency System, AIDS, is a viral disease, spread by bodily fluids, apparently not by kissing. Incubation does not affect health and takes eight years on average. There are then two phases, Human Immunodeficiency Virus, HIV, and ARC, Aids-related complex. The disease can stop at that point and disappear; but more commonly it develops into AIDS, with its life-expectancy of three years at most.

Alec Whitehead chose to cut short his terminal period.

Several quiet days, patients exceptionally thin on the ground, Ma visiting Jane in Norfolk, no word from Mary; but not a holiday, more like marking time, tension on the increase as we near the end of our month which bears a secular resemblance to Lent, the celebration of the fast in the wilderness.

I wrote too soon. Yesterday evening at about ten o'clock I received a telephone call. The caller began it thus: 'Joe...' The voice was female, tremulous, a sort of cry. I refrained from asking, 'Who is it?' – my heart was telling me. 'It's Mary,' she said, and I replied, 'I know.'

Those Christian names, let alone my nickname, how aphrodisiacal they are! Modern English manners, which scarcely use surnames, have stolen one of the great thrills once reserved for lovers.

'Melanie's ill,' Mary said.

'Shall I come out to you?'

'Could you?'

'Of course.'

'Do you know the way?'

'Of course. I'll be with you in fifteen minutes.'

It was a rush. I had to fetch medicaments from the Surgery. Then I drove flat-out through the roads and lanes, past the Forest of Ashes, and in through white wooden gates, along a gravelled drive, and stopped in a turning circle in front of a house with Gothic-style windows. A light was on above a Gothic front door, and electric light emanated through drawn curtains.

I rang the doorbell, and the door was immediately opened by a grey-haired elderly lady who said, 'Madam's upstairs.' I was in a staircase hall, and now Mary called down from above in a beckoning tone, 'Joe...' I mounted the stairs, met her at the top, and followed her into a large pretty bedroom with full-scale dressing-table and mirrors and a single bed, on which Melanie lay wheezing.

Mary said, 'She's a little better,' and Melanie tried to smile at me.

I gave her an inhaler and the mildest sedative, I did not want to frighten her with hypodermic syringes and oxygen masks – she was already on the mend. I talked to her as reassuringly as I could, putting my finger on my lips when she looked like talking. After five minutes or so she was breathing almost normally. I told her I would leave the room with her mother, in order that she could be quiet and settle down, but we would remain close by until we were sure she was okay. I happened to have brought a buzzer, which I put in her hand and explained that if she squeezed it we would hear the buzz.

Melanie is a sweet girl. She smiles through tears, and gradually was able to take deeper breaths. Her mother rearranged her pillows and sat on the edge of the bed smoothing her hair and stroking her forehead. Before too long her eyes were closing, and Mary and I left the room and sat together on a sofa on the landing – we were some ten yards from Melanie and the sounds of her breathing were audible through the open door.

Mary thanked me in an undertone, and I said to her: 'I'm sorry you were worried. Melanie should be all right now. I hope she'll grow out of her asthma. She's in the care of a London doctor, I know, I remember, so I've been careful not to administer any controversial medicine. I could leave you more pills and a flask of oxygen, but I'd rather you rang me in the unlikely event of another crisis during the night.'

'Would you mind?' she asked.

'Not at all – I'm used to it – and Melanie's a more worthwhile patient than some – and I'd do anything to help you.'

Her eyes filled with tears, and she said: 'I feel responsible.'

'For Melanie's asthma? God's responsible for that.'

She produced a handkerchief, dabbed at her eyes, said sorry, and then: 'Not God's fault this time.'

I was surprised, but had no sense of being in the vicinity of quicksand. Although she was wrought up, and had reason as a mother to be so, she was fundamentally composed, poised, and her composure transferred itself to me. There was an intimacy between us, and assurance that we could solve problems.

'What happened?'

'Her father frightened her.'

'How?'

'They're close, you see – she loves him, and I think he loves her.'

'Do you want to tell me what he did?'

'He put on a balaclava helmet.'

'What?'

'He wore it for skiing in his youth. It's knitted and dark blue and has holes for eyes and a mouth and covers the whole head. They were used by soldiers in the Crimean War, used for warmth. Bruce pretended to be a criminal when he went in to kiss Melanie good night.'

'Not a good joke.'

'No. I don't understand him any more.'

'Where is he now?'

'I don't know. He was upset by the screams and then the asthma. He might have driven back to London.'

'Are you going to be alone in the house?'

'No – Ursula's with me – she looks after us all – she began by helping me with the children – she let you in when you rang the bell.'

'Is Melanie in your bedroom?'

'Yes.'

'Where will you sleep?'

'With her – in there – in a big armchair – if I sleep; but that doesn't matter.'

'May I ask you one personal question?'

'Yes.'

'Can you cope with your husband?'

'I'm not frightened of him. He has a better side. He's changed a lot.'

'The month you asked for – you remember? – that month still has days to run.'

'I know,' she said. 'I turned to you because you're a doctor, but I would turn to you if I was in any trouble.'

'That's music to my ears, but ... But could we meet sometimes anyway? We still have to talk about *War and Peace*.'

'Yes ... Yes ...'

'You'll have to contact me.'

'Yes.'

'Will you?'

'Yes.'

'Thank you so much, Mary.'

'No – thank you – you've made such a difference for me.'

'Same here.'

'Perhaps . . .'

'All right, I'll leave you. I'll let myself out of the house. Ring if you need me.'

We stood up. She held out her hand and I clasped it in both of mine. Then I walked downstairs carrying my medicine chest and out into the night. I was glad she had not offered me only a cheek to kiss.

My recollections of Wisteria Lodge are vague – I did not have architectural matters on my mind. A light shone over a front door in two parts – the Gothic doorway and windows were probably Victorian. The house is family size, and no doubt the greenery clinging to the façade is wisteria. The hall was wide; doors opened into rooms right and left; the landing where I sat with Mary was a square space; and her bedroom had a high ceiling.

The single bed was of extreme interest to me. Considering that the Roecliffes were hardly middle-aged, and she was so desirable and he was unable to keep his hands to himself even at a dinner party, that bed must tell a sad story, but I was not crying.

My account of the episode is abridged. It cuts out or anyway loses the full romance of the long-awaited call in the late evening, the arrival at her home, admission into it by the traditional abigail, the ailing daughter and my successful attempt to ease suffering, and then our talk on

172

the landing, hushed, grateful, my reward, her beauty that was mine for the moment, her compliments and pledges, and the myriad implications.

The sequence of scenes had perspective and depth created by the shadows cast by Bruce Roecliffe. He was there, with us, in every way except in person. He was the agent of the summons I received, he had scared Melanie. His cruelty was the agency of our kinder acts. I hurried to his house, to treat his daughter, for the sake of his wife – I was the puppet on his string.

At my age and in my profession, as a reader and a student of the social comedy, I had theoretical knowledge of the eternal triangle, the *ménage à trois*. I knew it all when I first looked into Mary's quiet eyes in my consulting room, knew that she beckoned me from beyond the obstacles and thornbushes, the razor wire and minefields, barring the distance between us. Now, it would be almost as difficult to turn back as to carry on, setting aside the fact that I have no inclination or intention to change direction. Yet practically, in practice, I continually seem to touch the electrified wire that is Mary's marriage. She belongs to Bruce, and one of the links in the chain of my love of her, which she may or may not reciprocate, is that I do too.

Mrs Symonds, who enjoys ill health, brought me a sort of bouquet this morning, a fungal infection of a toenail, an irritable bowel, a suspected carbuncle, and a tic or twitch of her left eyelid that makes people think she is winking at them.

Old Sam Thomson, in my consulting room this a.m., cried despite his fighting fitness. His wife Nelly had been ill – cancer, chemotherapy. Tears were his response to strain. He has been so worried about Nelly, and he cannot believe she is cured. What is worse for him is that she refuses to 'take care of herself'. She does not let him do the housework or the shopping, apparently she does not go to bed early or get up late in the morning or sit still in between. He spoke of women in bitter-sweet terms. 'There's no controlling them for their own good, they won't be protected, not they. I see her running herself into trouble again, and I can't stop her.' I comforted and calmed him down as best I could. I referred him to a priest. But in my heart I was agreeing with him. Iris was a proud career girl, who would not brook 'protection' or 'interference' from the man she slept with. I never saw myself as a bridegroom standing by Iris attired in a virginal white dress before a priest and an altar. My daughter's death might have been my fault because I postponed an offer to marry her mother, and as a result Iris, in spite of her feminist attitudes or owing to her pride, rushed to have the abortion, which led to the parting of our ways and tears all round. I pine to protect Mary, but I know she would not let me, not yet, if ever.

Another extraordinary occurrence. I write in the evening – it is evening, nine days after my time at Wisteria Lodge – and this afternoon I had visitors, the Roecliffe family, minus Mary. Yes, Bruce came to call. Melanie and Tom were with him. I was taken unawares and aback – I had been having a nap in the chair beside my new wood-burning stove.

'Are we disturbing you?' he asked.

'No,' I lied.

He sat in the chair I had been sitting in – symbolical, since I had sat on his furniture in his home, including the bed he might have shared with Mary notwithstanding its single dimensions.

The children stayed close to him, touching, leaning on him, affectionately maybe, but they reminded me of the young offspring of predators, stroking and wheedling their parents who might be tempted to eat them.

'We're here to thank you for saving Melanie's bacon,' he said.

Melanie squirmed a little at this description, and Tom giggled rather sycophantically to please his father.

'You know my Melanie, have you met Tom? Let me introduce you – Doctor Selaby, Thomas Roecliffe – shake hands with the doctor, Tom – don't disgrace me!'

The boy shyly extended a limp moist hand: why was he sweating, why was he so nervous? They are fine-looking children, Tom handsome, his sister pretty, but pale – they are pale-faces, reserved, restricted. She has her asthmatic tendency, what is the matter with him?

Bruce was saying: 'Melanie's womanly, she'll marry young and have issue – you understand "issue", don't you, darling? She sides with her mother. Tom's a tomboy, he likes to kill things – we shoot sparrows with our catapults, don't we, Tom? He's going to have a gun soon and we'll shoot pigeons in the Forest of Ashes. He's a chip off my block, we're bloodthirsty.'

He was not exactly informing me, he was addressing his children and teasing them. They were noticeably unresponsive. They looked as if they had gone limp.

I offered them refreshments, and Bruce refused on their behalf: 'I won't have them growing up to be nuisances.' I then initiated them into the mysteries of my stove, which can run hot on maximum draught and many logs, and on minimum draught burn a single log for many hours. I next suggested that they might like to look around my house – for a start I indicated the staircase behind a cupboard door winding to the upper floors.

When Bruce and I were alone he said quite viciously: 'I'll tell you one thing about children, you can't do right in their bloody little eyes.'

I said I had neither children nor wife, and he commented: 'I envy you,' which was a bit hard to take considering that I wished his wife was mine. He continued: 'You don't need a wife to be lumbered with children – women are so bloody casual.'

I referred to the dinner at the Cunninghams', but he seemed to have forgotten it, he ignored me and said: 'How do I pay you for turning out to cosset my daughter in the middle of the night?'

I corrected his errors: 'Melanie was in pain and in danger, I administered suitable treatment, there was no cossetting, and your wife called me out at approximately ten p.m.'

'Okay, but how much?'

'I don't practice privately, and I don't know the NHS rate for a night-call, and I won't accept money for this one – expect further calls to be pricey.'

'Fair enough! What about that dinner party? I lashed out over the port, I was tight and bored – did I cut you to the quick?'

'No.'

'What a pity! I meant to let off a bomb under the Welfare State, which you lot collude with and support.'

'I support it unwillingly – I'm not in favour of change. You said that medical staff shouldn't tolerate the bad behaviour in A and Es at weekends. I agree. I agree wholeheartedly.' He showed no sign of appreciating my reference to himself. 'And,' I continued, 'I'm inclined to agree that we should isolate the drunks and druggers until they sober up and until proper patients have received treatment.'

'In great discomfort – concrete floor, concrete benches, one lavatory and unisex.'

'Well – warnings would have to be issued and

widely publicised. St Anne's Hospital in Tinbury would have to see the point, the police ditto, and money would have to be raised for a poster campaign and so on.'

'I'd contribute.'

'Thank you. I'll see if I can set the ball rolling.'

The children reappeared. They approved of my home – children like people and things to be their size. Their approval was expressed more by wan smiles than by words. Tom tried to explain to his father that the attic room was reached by a ladder, not stairs, and his father showed impatience with the halting delivery by turning his head away and frowning. Bruce is good-looking and so on, yet it struck me, when his cheek caught the light through my sitting-room window, that his skin is not a good colour under the suntan: wishful thinking?

'Come on, kids,' he said, standing up abruptly.

The 'kids' jarred on me: I object to inverted snobbery, people who talk common for effect, and I plead guilty to being a pedant – a kid is a young goat, and its parents are a billy and a nanny.

He opened my front door and stood on the pavement. I held my door open, and the children were behind me.

'If you've got any money to invest, contact me,' he said.

He was entitled to say so, he is a businessman, but I have inside information about his business. And I must add to my descriptions of his eyes: I would apply an adjective to them as metaphorical as that which describes Mary's eyes, his are 'hot', indicative of inner fires and dishonesty.

'Shake hands,' he said to Melanie, although he had not offered me a handshake.

Another limp hand touched mine.

I said, 'Goodbye, Melanie,' and she glanced at me fugitively and mumbled thanks.

Tom said to me when we shook hands: 'I don't think your house is poor.'

At evening surgery yesterday, a couple of hours after Bruce and the two Roecliffe children had left me, James Bolt brought his son Jimmy into my consulting room. James is a smallholder, he and his wife Aggie grow asparagus and other unusual vegetables on a few acres near Clayburn. Jimmy is nine, red-checked and sturdy. He is a cricketer, had been batting, and received a bouncer that connected with his temple rather than his bat. He told me: 'I was trying to hit the ball to square leg, but it swung in and caught me.' The boy was amused, his father worried by the egg-shaped swelling: 'Is it okay?' he asked me. My advice was to take the casualty home, get Aggie to put a cold compress on the bruise and a bandage, then early to bed and, if the swelling had not subsided by the next morning, more medical examination. Jimmy was pleased not to be fussed over. He thanked me for not giving him an injection and shook my hand hard. He and his father went away laughing. They made me feel sorrier for Melanie and Tom.

* * *

Supper with Ma. She is concerned about Lisbet Tinnislea, who has fallen mysteriously ill and is losing weight. Her doctor is called Hemming and belongs to the other practice in Maeswell, and in Ma's opinion is hopeless. I could not ethically, and would not like to, step in for all Ma's urging. Bruce is Lisbet's friend, he might help her.

At last – at least it seemed to me to be at last – a call from Mary.
'Can we discuss *War and Peace*?'
'When?'
'Now.'
'I'm waiting.'
She arrived. We looked at each other in a way that was better than shaking hands or a mutual peck. She excites and calms me simultaneously. We began with the refrain of the song of love:
'Are you all right? ... Are you?'
'Come and sit down!'
'I can't stay long.'
'Is Melanie dancing?'
'And Tom's in the gym.'
She continued: 'I'm not here because Bruce was, I'm not following in his footsteps.'
'I hoped you weren't.'
'What was he like? I didn't know he was planning to visit.'
'He was pleasant. I've no complaints.'
'He can be pleasant.'

'He was not so pleasant at the Cunninghams'.'

'I know that.'

'But he made a suggestion there – we discussed it the other day – it's about the management of the A and E at St Anne's Hospital.'

'Where you treated his dislocated finger?'

'Exactly.'

'I'm not meant to know that – he's kept it dark. Never mind! You're not getting involved in a business venture with Bruce?'

'Oh no.'

'Don't, don't – I don't want you to be involved – it'd be a great mistake.'

'I won't – I'm well aware of what a mistake it would be – and because of my friendship with you.'

'Yes … Yes … I must talk to you…'

'Likewise!'

She laughed, we both did – our conversation was like gliding over a surface of humour, good humour, notwithstanding its urgency and gravity.

She said: 'My marriage isn't normal – I mean it's open to some extent – but not really for me. Our friendship, yours and mine, might become difficult.'

'I expect so.'

'No – more difficult than you expect – Bruce is a strange person – I don't understand him after being his wife in name for many years – he ties everything and everybody in knots.'

'Does he know you're here?'

'No.'

'Is it difficult for you to meet me like this?'

'No – easy, lovely, but complicated – my marriage – I couldn't leave Bruce, not even completely emotionally – I owe him a debt, and have to accept his waywardness and faithlessness.'

'Is Melanie his daughter?'

'Tom's his son.'

'I see.'

'You see so much, but not the whole picture. I wonder if anyone in the world sees into Bruce's heart, or if he has one. No matter! I shouldn't meet you for your sake.'

'Not true!'

'I'm sure to disappoint you.'

'Nobody can take decisions for another person.'

'I came to say...'

'You haven't said it, I can't hear it. Listen to me! I'm forty-one years of age. I had a mistress for a long time, but it's over and done with. I'm not promiscuous, I never have been, and have loads of experience, I know myself and my own mind. When I met you something irreversible happened to me. I'm sorry, I'll try not to be a drag on you, but there it is – I'm a healthy man, but I'd rather love you near or far than compromise elsewhere.'

'Oh dear ... Oh, my dear...'

'That sounds nice.'

'We hardly know each other.'

'I've known you well enough ever since we met, and perhaps before.'

'You're saying wonderful and terrible things.'

'I'm rushing in, yet I'm not an absolute fool. Where are you going?'

'To fetch my children.'

'It's too soon.'

'I'm wrong to sit with you.'

'Not very.'

'I've told you anyway – I've put you first – think of it – remember!'

'You're a beautiful woman, Mary, beautiful through and through, and adorable and exciting.'

'I'm stopping my ears!'

'Well, listen again – take your hands away from your ears! I shan't talk to you so frankly again, unless you wish it. Can't you stay a little longer?'

'I don't dare. Goodbye, Joe. How does your door open?'

I stood up and opened the door. We stood facing each other for a moment. She leant forward and touched my lips with hers, then hurried down the street without looking back.

Thanks be for her contrariness!

But which is meaningful, the goodbye or the kiss?

I can see the outline of the tale of Mary, Melanie and Bruce, and could have a shot at colouring in the rest, the fears and tears, the ceasefires and the resumption of hostilities, the relief, the regrets. I bow my head to Mary, who behaved better than me. She sacrificed herself rather than her child, assuming that it was a sacrifice for her to marry Bruce.

* * *

Winter is on the way, season of colds, coughs and pointless consultations, heydays of hypochondriacs and self-obsessed neurotics, fatal for some and not good for the doctors still on their feet who have to shoulder the extra burden of colleagues on sick leave. Moreover, night falls early, mothers in general are not keen to drive their children anywhere in the dark, and one mother in particular may not take her little girl to dancing lessons and her son to gym in the late afternoon. Will we ever get down to *War and Peace*?'

This notebook is a new 'economy' format, it has half as many pages more than the other four notebooks – a bargain, the makers proclaim, although the price seems higher. I doubt that I will use the extra pages. My life is again in the doldrums, nothing is worthy of record.

In the rest-room at the Surgery, I spoke my piece about the mayhem at weekends at St Anne's, and our possible response in order to ameliorate it or at least to provide protection for the medicos on duty. It was a flop, no takers, and in fact Denis Woods disappeared before I had finished speaking. Frank Cunningham was dead against the incarceration, the kidnapping, however temporary, of drunkards and others of that ilk. Police had powers to lock up offenders, doctors and nurses had none. He said that bad behaviour used to be the prerogative of the upper classes who could afford it, now the lower classes could afford their turn to make beasts of themselves. My proposal was illegal and impractical, he said, and he was surprised that I had advanced it. Audrey Fletcher shook the feminist tambourine at me: although she is strong for women's rights, and women doing men's jobs, she recoiled from the notion of drunken women having to use the unisex lavatory. Neither Frank nor Audrey are realistic. The former is too old for night duty at St Anne's, the latter as the mother of two young children is excused. I was at St Anne's last Saturday night from ten p.m. to two a.m. on Sunday morning. A youth screamed abuse at us for one and a half hours for not giving him drugs: in the end we forcibly administered a sedative. A nurse had her arm badly twisted, a porter was punched and stamped on. Natural functions took a lot of clearing up. I did not become a doctor to be a nursemaid and a punchbag for the aggressive new-rich on the razzle. The world has changed more than Frank and Audrey know: the laws of the land discriminate against law-abiding people – blinkered liberals and cock-eyed do-gooders are paving the way for an iron man, a martinet, a cruel despot and tyrant.

I suppose I feel under the weather because it rains non-stop, my country is badly governed and decadent, Ma has been unwell, I am lonely and have received no word from Mary Roecliffe.

Oh hell! I wish I was not about to write this

entry – and I have to beg to differ from Tolstoy, the truth is not always beautiful. We have had four nice days, sunny, still, a saint's 'little summer', no doubt. This afternoon I decided not to wait for my telephone to ring, and went for a walk in the Forest of Ashes. I walked for about half an hour and was overcome with sleep, a result of my covering for Denis Woods who had taken Alyson and their children to the seaside for a holiday. I therefore branched off the ride and into the undergrowth, looking for a tree, an evergreen if possible, under which the earth would have been sheltered from rain. I found a hillock, a stony outcrop, part of which had once been quarried. The sun tempted me to climb to the top, and, although there was no shade and the ground was rock-hard, I lay down and shut my eyes. I slept for half an hour or so, and woke with a start – something had woken me, something that differed from the noises emitted by woodland birds and animals. It was laughter, male laughter, I thought; and it rose up from the ride below me. Two figures came into view, and one was Bruce Roecliffe. The other was a younger man or boy – I guessed at first that it was Tom: because a gun was hooked on Bruce's right forearm and a cartridge belt was round his waist, he must be going to teach Tom how to shoot. But then I saw that the second person was a man with a dark head of hair. One or both of them laughed again, and they turned into the undergrowth on that farther side of the ride. They were gone for six or seven minutes. When they reappeared, Bruce was tightening his cartridge belt and his companion held the gun. They walked on, Bruce again in possession of his gun, and passed out of sight. Later, as I gathered my wits about me and climbed down the hillock and headed for where I had left my car, I heard a gunshot.

No jumping to conclusions, I have told myself since then. The most acceptable explanation is that Bruce and his pal were out to shoot pigeons.

My notes will have to end here. It has passed the time for me to jot them down. The personal stuff I shall burn or shred at some stage. No word from Mary for nearly a month – I fear she is in trouble, also that I could make matters worse. Perhaps we have both needed time to ourselves. The future is dark.

No stopping after all – fate dictates and I do as I am told.

Mary and I met by accident in Wates' pharmacy, and I brought her to The Poor Cottage. She looked pale and fragile. When I shut the door we faced each other, I held out my arms and she fell into them with her head on my shoulder. Our embrace was emotional rather than sexual, if love acknowledges such a division. She broke away and sat on the chair opposite mine by the stove.

'I've tried so hard not to do this,' she said.

'Thank heaven you haven't succeeded.'

'My farewell hasn't lasted long.'

'Long enough, too long.'

'Maybe.'

'Are you sorry to have failed?'

She laughed.

'Is someone not well?' I asked. 'You were in the chemist's.'

'Yes ... I don't know. Are you well?'

'Yes – I went to buy toothpaste. What does "don't know" mean?'

'I was buying vitamins for Bruce.'

'He hasn't seemed to me to need vitamins.'

'He's ill.'

'Really?'

'Off and on, he's been getting ill for ages.'

'What sort of ill?'

'That's what we don't know – fatigue, exhaustion, the opposite of his normal constitution.'

'Has he seen a doctor?'

'Oh yes – in London – but they can't find anything wrong – he says they can't. He's not a good patient, he doesn't like doctors, and he's quarrelsome when he's feeling bad.'

'Not good for you.'

'Would you see him?'

'Say that again?'

'Would you come to tea at Wisteria Lodge – today, a social visit – I could explain how we met – and you could give me your opinion – you wouldn't have to examine Bruce or do any doctoring?'

I put forward excuses. But she pleaded with

me, she had no time to listen to my arguments, and I agreed to do as she wished.

We drove in the gloaming to Wisteria Lodge, she in her white Ford Fiesta, self in my Golf, and parked on the gravel sweep in front of the Gothic front door and windows. Melanie and Tom came out of the sitting-room to greet us in the hall. Mary asked Melanie to look after me, then went towards the back of the house. The sitting-room was brightly lit, and cheerful with the children's toys on the floor. Melanie wanted me to play cards with her, pontoon otherwise known as blackjack, and Tom showed me his model cars, a Bugatti with exhaust pipes extending from the bonnet and a gull-wing Mercedes. The children were more relaxed and chatty than ever before. After about ten minutes Mary returned and signalled to me from the doorway.

I told the children I was wanted elsewhere, and said quietly to Mary: 'If he doesn't want to see me I don't think I should barge in.'

'He's ready for you,' she replied, 'but he won't be cooperative.'

'Shall we call it off?'

'No – please,' she said, 'for me.'

I followed her along a passage and into an office.

She addressed her husband who sat in a big black leather reclining chair: 'Here's Dr Selaby, Bruce.'

The door closed behind me. Bruce offered me a chair on my side of the desk. The setting was dramatic: curtains drawn, illumination mostly by the winking screens of computers, one anglepoise standard lamp casting light on the black leather throne in or on which Bruce sat crumpled, wearing an open-necked shirt and red cardigan.

'This wasn't my idea,' he said with a wry and uncharacteristically feeble smile.

'Can I help you at all or would you like me to get out of your sight?'

'The latter, but not for a minute.'

I waited and he resumed: 'Okay – I'm sometimes grounded by a bloody bug – there was one doctor in London with a brain, he kept me on my feet without any fuss – I can't prescribe for myself – are you prepared to play ball?'

'What are your symptoms?'

'I'm not going into that.'

'Well, I'll leave you in peace.'

'Don't do that! I'm run-down and my stomach's not right in the present instance.'

'Have there been other instances?'

'Some.'

'Have you had tests?'

'I've had a few, and don't intend to have any more.'

'What did the brainy doctor do for you?'

'He cured me.'

'How?'

'With a hell of an antibiotic.'

'What was it called?'

'God knows.'

'Sorry – I'm not playing. Why not go back to the doctor who cured you?'

'He's turned up his toes, he was old and he's left me dangling.'

'You could try to find a doctor who's more amenable than I am.'

'I'm not in a fit state to find anybody or anything – can't you see?'

'My advice is to go for tests.'

'Clever you! You've made me feel a lot worse, Doctor.'

'Good night – good luck!'

I left the room, and met Mary in the passage.

'Did you hear any of our conversation?' I asked.

'I couldn't hear.'

'He should have tests.'

'Did you suggest them?'

'Yes.'

'What happened?'

'He more or less pointed to the door.'

'I'm sorry.'

'I did it for you. I'd do more than this for you.'

'Thank you. I must go into him – he won't like to think he's being discussed. Can I talk to you?'

'Any time.'

'About Bruce.'

'I understand – not *War and Peace*.'

'Good night.'

She kissed me again, fleetingly, gratefully, and turned away before I had a chance to make much contribution.

I headed for the sitting-room and said goodbye

to the children. They wanted me to stay – they too wanted me to play – but I again refused, this time regretfully – and returned to The Poor Cottage, feeling upset for lots of reasons.

It must have been the day after when I spoke to Denis Woods. I pushed one of my upsetting reasons to a logical conclusion, and detained Denis in the rest-room after evening surgery.

'Can I ask you a hypothetical favour?' I began.

'You can, but I reserve the right not to give you the answer you're hoping for,' he replied.

Did he know the Roecliffes?

By name, he thought there was a pretty wife, and had an idea they lived near Taylton.

I said: 'Bruce Roecliffe's unwell, he may be ill, I've advised tests, and he may or may not agree to follow my advice. I'm not his doctor, I've treated one of his two children, a girl with asthma, and I'm friendly with his wife. If Bruce should wish to sign on with our Practice, would you accept him as a patient?'

'What's the catch?'

'I couldn't and wouldn't be Mary Roecliffe's doctor, owing to our friendship, and therefore couldn't be Bruce's. He's a bit of an awkward customer, a freelance financier, and he spreads it about.'

'Does "spreading it about" mean what I think it means?'

'Probably.'

'You're not asking Audrey to be his hypothetical doctor?'

'Certainly not.'

'How ill is he?'

'I can't say – my interview with him lasted four minutes in a half-dark room, and we didn't shake hands. He's not a nobody, he's an interesting man.'

'To wish an interesting patient on a doctor sounds like a Chinese curse.'

'Hypothetically, Denis, in the unlikely event of Bruce being sensible, will you do it?'

'I will,' he replied: 'and I haven't said "I will" since I married.'

As a result, I wrote with relief to Bruce – calling him by his first name as I used Mary's – to hope he was better, to clarify my professional position, and inform him that Dr Denis Woods, my experienced colleague, would be ready to offer assistance if need be.

Frank Cunningham, our senior partner, was not involved in these proceedings. I had been afraid that he would not allow Bruce to curse and swear at doctors in our Surgery.

Waiting for a bomb to fall in your vicinity is not the most pleasant of pastimes. I visited Ma again: it was late evening, when I was less expectant of a particular telephone call. Ma had had flu, a nasty strain of it, but was now convalescent. She thanked me for having been so attentive, and I thanked her for having been a good mother to me. I privately thank heaven for both my parents. I have personal experience of the opposite, not only in connection with

Mary's children, but some of my patients with theirs. Everything costs something, what you do and fail to do will cost you, and the price of procreation should not be borne by innocent and uninvolved other people.

Mary was with me for nearly an hour: Melanie and Tom were at their classes. She asked me what was wrong with Bruce, and I had no answer – his only symptom I was told about could be caused by any number of diseases, some more serious than others. I asked if he was still suffering from digestive trouble and exhaustion, and then if he had had constructive second thoughts on tests: her answers were yes and no.

It was our most emotional meeting. I could not conceal my mingled joy and anxiety at seeing her again, and she made no secret of her sighs of relief to be in my arms. We had embraced as lovers do in the lull of a storm.

She said: 'I owe you explanations, I've broken my word twice now, by calling for your help and by coming here again. I didn't mean to. I couldn't help it. I need to explain my marriage so far as I can, and if possible spare you sorrow.'

I found it hard to listen to her, I was distracted by her voice, way of speaking, movements of her lips, expressions, gestures. She said she had been orphaned, her father perishing in the army in a war, her mother dying of TB when she was twelve. She lived then with an aunt and uncle in Shropshire. She went through college and she landed a job in a finance house. A man did her wrong and left her to cope with her pregnancy.

She said: 'I was ready to rear my child, my aunt understood my predicament and my uncle would have helped with money, but Bruce had a different idea. He was a friend of Melanie's father. He was a star turn at that time, launching his own business, handsome and surrounded by girls. He offered to marry me out of the blue. We were not lovers and scarcely friends. He said a good deed would be the making of him, he called himself rotten and a lost soul, and I imagined the task of remodelling him was worthwhile. We married in a Register Office, not church, and it was all on impulse and convenient for me, I admit. Problems took over at once. He was eccentric. He was forgivable, but his promises weren't kept. I conceived Tom, and things got worse. Bruce paid me less and less attention, he had other interests, and I made an unwelcome discovery Our marital life ended there. I would have left, but he persuaded me not to, and I stayed on partly for the sake of the children and partly to support him. He seemed to be cursed. He wasn't well, although his spells of ill health were short-lived. He was moody, yet had redeeming features, his dependence on me, his guilt and unhappiness. I couldn't leave him. I can't. I don't know if you would ever want me to leave. I don't presume, but my conscience has nagged for not telling you outright that all I have to offer is friend-ship. Bruce must be iller than he or anyone else knows, and I have loyalties that refuse to be divided.'

My paraphrase is the gist of her story. None of it cooled my ardour. I admired her honesty, and even her scruples. That she was cognisant of the range of Bruce's sexual antics, and I did not have to add to her burdens with my suspicion, was a weight off my mind. In my turn I made my confession, trying not to speak ill of Iris or too emotionally of Rose. I emphasised that my feelings for Iris were nothing like my feelings for herself, nothing whatsoever.

Before she left I asked her if Bruce had mentioned my letter about Denis Woods, and told her what was in it and why I had written.

She answered no, and said that Bruce was extremely secretive.

Schizophrenia beckons. Manic-depression is round the corner. I swing between optimism and pessimism, lightheartedness and gloom. Denis is another secretive man, he does not discuss his patients publicly, and I dare not dig for information about Bruce Roecliffe. At any rate the 'understanding' that Mary and I have arrived at is a lovely thing.

Is the news good? Is the news bad? It has reached me from an unexpected quarter. Ma tells me that she was told by Gabriella Shelby that Bruce Roecliffe has submitted to tests and been given a clear bill of health. I am sceptical – Ma said I was too much so. And I have to be glad for his sake, for Mary's, and contrarily for my own. I would not have liked to step into a dead man's shoes in a hurry. I am not altruistic or a saint: I foresaw pain for him and anguish for her, and possibly inextricable and insurmountable complications, which I no longer need to name or contemplate.

I wrote Mary a note to say how pleased I was to hear that Bruce had 'passed' his tests, and asking her to offer him my good wishes.

Months have passed. It is the next year. The short paragraph of a sentence above was to all intents and purposes my final note. But life has brought my story to a more recognisable end – coincidentally, my double notebook is running out of pages. What follows will be written not in the form of notes approximating to a journal, but like a narrative in a book.

I have to guess, since my notes were not dated, that it was a year ago when I congratulated Bruce Roecliffe and wished him well. My congratulations were premature. A few days after I heard that he had been given the all-clear, I received a call from Mary. She sounded agitated and was ringing me from London – I was at The Poor Cottage after evening surgery. She said Bruce was in a sort of hospital. He had suddenly developed a combination of symptoms almost simultaneously, in a matter of twenty-four hours, and had chosen to be treated by the successor of his old London doctor rather than by Dr Woods. He and she had been fetched by private ambulance, he was in the clinic where Dr Wolverton worked, and she was staying in their flat near Victoria Station. Bruce was awfully ill, she said, but well looked after, she believed, and she herself was okay – Melanie and Tom were with the abigail, Ursula, at Wisteria Lodge. Apart from letting me know what had happened and where she was, and wanting to hear my voice, she wondered if I would explain things with apologies to Denis Woods.

Two days later she rang me in tears: Bruce had AIDS.

I still know very little about the disease. In the case of Alec Whitehead, my treatment consisted of a single consultation and a prescription for pain-killers. When I saw Bruce in the grip of fatigue it crossed my mind that he with his equivocal libido might have contracted HIV, the precursor of AIDS. But there were many possible causes of his thin neck and bony hands. I could not bear to think of the effects of AIDS on his wife, my Mary, her children and maybe many other people.

Mary's second call to me, the tearful one, confirmed my fears. She asked for information, she begged me to tell her the truth. I knew enough to be able to describe the stages of the development of AIDS, first HIV, which could become ARC, AIDS related complex, and finally the disease itself. Round about the transition from HIV to ARC there was a chance of the infection disappearing: Bruce's constitution might be able to seize such a chance.

'But...' she said, between a question and a statement.

One 'but', I replied, was that I had to ask her whether she had ever experienced an unusual symptom, and, if she would forgive me, selfishly for my peace of mind, and less selfishly for her own protection, when she had last had sexual relations with Bruce.

'Ages ago,' she sobbed.

'You understand my question?'

'Yes.'

'How long has it been?'

'Not since I was pregnant with Tom.'

'How old is Tom?'

'Nine and a half.'

'Ten years since you slept with Bruce?'

'This is painful, Joe.'

'For both of us.'

'He wanted me in other ways – I was essential – but always expected him to leave me – and I had the children – and wasn't happy. Sorry – I'll try again – yes, ten years.'

'And symptoms?'

'I've never been ill.'

'Thank God!'

'Why? How long is the incubation period?'

'I believe the average age is eight or nine years.'

'Tom...'

'Tom can't have AIDS if he hasn't been ill already – children develop it in months rather than years.'

'Are you sure, Joe?'

I took a risk and answered in the affirmative.

A little later I asked, 'How's Bruce?' and apologised for remembering the invalid belatedly.

'He's not surprised. He was HIV for a long time – he never told me – I was oblivious – and he's been afraid it had turned into AIDS. The disease accounts for a lot, but I can't say that knowing he was ill would have made our marriage easier. Now I'm sorry to see him so unlike himself. Thank you, Joe – please understand me. Now I must go back to the clinic, I promised I would.'

Soon after that conversation Mary returned to Wisteria Lodge – Bruce sent her back to be with the children. She travelled up to London and down again every few days for a month or two. We met, she came to The Poor Cottage, but we were discreet, we were equally keen not to be the subject of gossip while her husband was stricken. Moreover, we were careful not to discuss a hypothetical future: we stuck to practical subjects like the children's schooling and Bruce's pills.

Eventually, in confidence, I informed Denis Woods of his potential patient's condition, and conveyed the Roecliffes' apologies. He said he had wondered if AIDS might be the villain of the piece. What about the all-clear, I asked. He replied that mistakes are sometimes made when the disease is in its formative ARC phase.

Bruce improved slightly, and Mary was adjusting to the situation so far as was possible.

But subsidiary troubles befell the Roecliffes, and I was powerless to shelter the innocent one from their impact.

Ma was the first agent to bring a consequence of Bruce's sickness to my attention. I called on her at Silver Court one evening and guessed she had something on her mind.

She began by saying, 'Lisbet Tinnislea's not at all well.'

I mumbled a word of sympathy.

'She's supposed to have a ghastly disease.'

'Oh?'

'It's name is initials, HIV. That's serious, isn't it?'

'Yes.'

'Is it like AIDS?'

'It can become AIDS, but can also disappear.'

'Well, it isn't disappearing. Is it fatal, Joe?'

'HIV isn't, AIDS used to be and still is often; but they're working on a cure and they'll find one before too long.'

'Lisbet's seventy and sinking. A cure in the future probably won't help. She's such a nice dear person.'

'I'm sorry, Ma.'

'She's told us she knows how she caught it.'

'How is that?'

'From the husband of your friend, Joe.'

'I don't think that's possible.'

'Bruce Roecliffe visited her to talk about the money he was going to invest, and they had an affair. It happened at their only meeting. She hasn't known any other man since she lost her husband. Now she's heard that Bruce is dying of AIDS, and she believes she is, too.'

'When is the affair supposed to have occurred?'

201

'Nine years ago. She was always pretty, you see, and generous.'

'And truthful?'

'Oh yes, truthful and not fanciful. You needn't think that her age makes the story unlikely. Bruce Roecliffe came to see Gabriella Shelby about money and tried to have an affair with her – and Gabriella's much older now than Lisbet was then.'

Again I commiserated.

Ma said: 'Anyway, why I'm telling you is that Lisbet wrote to Bruce Roecliffe and his wife answered her letter. Mary Roecliffe wrote back so kindly, poor woman, and the message from Bruce she conveyed was a comfort to Lisbet.'

On another occasion another consequence was revealed to me and to Audrey Fletcher in the rest-room at the Surgery.

Frank Cunningham referred to Bruce's AIDS and told us that David Havior was HIV-positive and in hospital. David was the surviving son, and last presumptive heir to the ancient Havior barony: he must also have been the younger man I saw with Bruce in the Forest of Ashes. Apparently old Lady Havior, Helen, who lives in Maeswell, was always against David's friendship with Bruce, and had now written a furious letter to both Roecliffes, accusing them of ruining her family. Frank explained that if or when David died the Haviors would be done for emotionally, also financially, since there would be a second charge of death duty to pay, and because their name would be extinct. Frank then asked if Audrey and I would assure Mary Roecliffe, if we had a chance, that David might have picked up the infection elsewhere, and bring them round to believing as he did that she had nothing to blame herself for.

His revelations did not stop there. Shell Perry was HIV, he said, and the dermatologist blamed Bruce and was divorcing her.

'It's a bad business,' Frank wound up, 'but we doctors aren't judges.'

The third and last of the consequences I heard about was less bad than the others – at least Mary was not dragged into it. A Mrs Munsley with son aged two booked an appointment with me. A new receptionist had taken the booking and knew nothing except the name of the lady. Mrs Munsley wearing a hat, dark glasses and a scarf wheeled in a pushchair and disrobed to the extent of uncovering the Nicky Benning of yore. We embraced. She cried. What was wrong? She was scared. She was friends with a nurse who worked for Dr Wolverton in the clinic where Bruce Roecliffe was treated for AIDS. She had spent a weekend with Bruce, two nights in Brighton, long before she and I nearly got together, before she worked at St John's Surgery: how much at risk was she? She had a beautiful son, Timmy, and a great husband – they were all happy – she was a reformed character, she had married in church – was she, was her son, was her husband, in danger? She had AIDS hanging over her head and theirs. She had come to see me secretly, hoping no one would recognise her.

Was there anything she could do? What should and could she do? How was she to recognise a symptom?

I answered her questions as best I could. She had youth and strength on her side, Timmy ditto, and her looks did not pity her. Should the necessity arise, there was an AIDS specialist not far from where she was living.

'Come and see me again in a few years,' I said, and she hugged me goodbye and went away bravely.

Meanwhile the planet continued to spin. Bruce was still in London, Mary visited him, and when she was absent I spent afternoons at Wisteria Lodge, playing games with Melanie and Tom. I played tennis with Melanie and cricket with Tom, and cards and Monopoly with both, and we ate teas produced by Ursula. Melanie benefited from Bruce's absence, the longer he was absent the more she relaxed and came out of her shell, and Tom too seemed increasingly carefree – the gun with which he had been going to shoot pigeons was not mentioned. I enjoyed their company, they reminded me of their mother, and they were less boring than the majority of children of their ages. We discussed their schools and schooling, their likes, dislikes and plans, and somehow skirted round the subject of Bruce.

One day at Wisteria Lodge, Mary arrived back from London just as I was leaving. We had a moment together in private, and she said that Bruce had expressed a wish to see me. I could not refuse.

He had been in and out of the clinic, and on the occasion of my visit was in his London flat and Mary was in the country. The flat was on the 'ground' floor – up steps but with other flats above it – of an Edwardian purpose-built block. A nurse was in attendance, she let me in and escorted me into the front room, which must have been the sitting-room. The time was between six and seven o'clock – I had skipped evening surgery. Curtains were drawn, the room was dark except for an extendable reading lamp on a table by the bed on which Bruce lay – furniture had been pushed aside and stacked to create space. He was propped up on pillows. The beam of the lamp was directed away from him – I could only see a half-lit profile of his face. He had a colourful scarf round his neck and wore dark blue pyjamas, and was smart even if his head was skeletal and he kept his arms and hands under the covers.

His voice was low and his breathing difficult. He greeted me by saying, 'My dear chap!' I spoke to him and waited.

'Find a chair,' he said, and after another pause, 'Sorry for the heat and gloom, eyes and circulation not what they used to be.'

I sat down where he might be able to see me. We talked as I remember, he taking the lead.

'How are you, Doctor?'

'Well, I think.'

'That's the spirit, not to be too sure you're well. I'm the proof that pride comes before a fall. I thought it couldn't happen to me, and it wouldn't dare to turn nasty. Won't you have a drink? Ring that bell and my nurse will oblige – she might give you morphia if that's your fancy.'

I said I wanted nothing, and he was polite enough not to press me.

'Thank you for being kind to my children. I wasn't always kind to Melanie, and now she sends me cakes without poison in them, I'm told – I was never a cake-eater. She takes after her mother, she has a talent for tolerance, and she'll be another beauty one fine day. Give her my love. Give her confidence – I don't want her to think all men are as bad as I've been – but don't let her fall in love with you! Tom's a wax tablet – I haven't made too much impression on him, I hope, and Mary knows better than to bag all his affections. Let him be straight, for goodness sake! I wasn't cut out to be a father, more's the pity.'

'I've no children of my own, I'm not an expert in that line.'

'No, but ... I used to be rude about doctors, but I've revised my opinion, and I know for a fact that, in spite of all the pills you've prescribed, you haven't done a fraction of the damage that's down to yours truly. Are you aware of what I'm talking about?'

'Yes.'

'I'm haunted – I'm like Macbeth. You knew Nicky Benning, didn't you?'

'I've seen her recently.'

'Is she okay?'

'So far.'

206

'And other girls, other women, and not only women – too many, too many – have you seen them?'

'My mother's a friend of Lisbet Tinnislea.'

'She's ill, isn't she?'

'Yes.'

'Will you think of a suitable message from me to her?'

'Yes.'

' "Each man kills the thing he loves" – true words, aren't they?'

'Yes indeed.'

'I have, except for Mary – she escaped me, she resisted – the good in her was stronger than the bad in me. She believes I have a soul. It's my mind that's suspect. My disease affects the mind. But it's too late for excuses. Thank you for being Mary's friend.'

'I thank her for being mine.'

'You're right, you're lucky. I wasn't religious, I was a satyr; but, by God, if you catch AIDs you see the point of religion – you see it with a vengeance. No, that's a silly way of putting it – I mean, you appreciate the religion that's forgiving. I get tired quickly, which isn't a help to a host. Sorry...'

His voice trailed away and I thought he was asleep.

But he rallied, woke and said: 'I may go to America and get the medication that can cope. On the other hand, I may decide I don't deserve it. Who knows? I asked you here to give you my blessing – how ridiculous! – as if I had the right to bless you – but Mary values your friendship. Do you catch my meaning?'

'I think so.'

'Stand by her.'

'I will if she'll let me.'

'And if she won't?'

'I'll be there.'

'Thanks, Joe.'

There was a long pause. He was alive but no longer with me. I tiptoed out of the room.

There is room for one more note in notebook five.

I would never have chosen to be Bruce's friend, yet we are drawn ever closer – another unintended consequence. Not only do I love his wife, depend on him not to hurt or harm her, entertain his children, and obey the summons to visit him while he wrestles with death, but we are also linked by guilt. I killed Rose, he may have killed 'many'. We seek forgiveness. The advantages of the permissive society do not come cheap. The oaths Bruce and I swore, the laws of nature, the commandments of God, we got round them. We are chips off the block of the history of mankind. We did as we pleased and were licensed to do by science and fashion, atheism and amorality. We are the children of our forefathers who had inquiring minds and rebellious temperaments, Adam and Eve, for example.

Some days ago Ma asked me to visit her at Silver Court. She told me that Bruce had repaid the friend of the Cunninghams' whose money he had lost – the cheque was signed by Mary.

'Perhaps he had some good in him,' she remarked.

'He loved people in his fashion.'

'Is he dying?'

'I can't be sure, he seems to be.'

'If he died, how would it affect Mary?'

'Again I can't be sure.'

'And yourself, Joe?'

'I don't know.'

'How old is she?'

'Thirty-nine.'

'She could still have children.'

'Yes.'

'Will you wait for her for ever?'

'Please, Ma!'

'I'm sorry.'

'Don't be sorry for me.'

That day or the next I saw Mary, she came to The Poor Cottage. Her report was that Bruce had taken a positive turn, benefited from my visit, eaten food and talked of getting back to Wisteria Lodge as soon as his appearance would not alarm the children. I was congratulatory, notwithstanding the ultimate irony of my reviving my rival.

She said: 'I love you too much, Joe, to go on like this – I can't, I know I shouldn't – it's too awful.'

'It is awful.'

'What must your mother think of me!'

'Not relevant.'

'The disease can stretch out. There are new pills. Isn't that right?'

'Yes and no.'

'I can't say don't wait, I haven't the strength, but I think you should decide not to, I'm afraid you should. Honestly, Joe! Darling Joe, I'm being contrary, but you can read my mind. Tell me! Help me to read yours!'

'I won't tell you, but I will give you a present. Yes, a present, a small one. Ever since I arrived in this place, in The Poor Cottage, I've taken notes, not a diary, not *War and Peace*, just jottings. There are five notebooks now, and they tell the truth, our story, my side of our story, from when I got lost in your eyes in my consulting room. You remember, don't you? You've said something similar happened to you. Well, it's all here. You don't have to read my notebooks, but if you do you'll find my answer to the question of whether to wait or not to wait. They're my life in a manner of speaking, and they're for you.'